The
Star Namer
and the
Unchosen

To Stephanie. Geronimo

The
Star Namer
and the
Unchosen

Aim Higher!

Peggy Miracle Consolver

Peggy

Carpenter's Son Publishing

The Star Namer and the Unchosen

©2019 by Peggy Consolver

Published by Carpenter's Son Publishing, Franklin, Tennessee.

Published in association with Larry Carpenter of Christian Book Services, LLC.
www.christianbookservices.com

Cover and Interior Design by Suzanne Lawing

Edited by Lee Titus Elliott

Printed in the United States of America

978-1-949572-49-0

The Star Namer and the Unchosen

Is dedicated to the memory of
Eskie Newberry Miracle
Grandfather and original Appalachian
Storyteller of the family.

Consolver's Other Books

Shepherd, Potter, Spy—and the Star Namer (2015). This award-winning book introduced the family of the master potter of Gibeon. From twelve-year-old Keshub's point of view, the biblical drama of the invasion of Canaan by the Hebrews unfolded in eye-witness detail. You feel like you are there because the author *has been there.*

Digging Deeper into HIStory: A Study Guide for Shepherd, Potter Spy—and the Star Namer (2016) followed *Shepherd, Potter* . . . because the first book is actually "a Bible study masquerading as a novel." In this thirteen-unit booklet, the author shares some of the great stuff she learned while researching the novel, participating in an archaeological dig in Israel, and standing on the sites where the action happened. This interactive* Bible study is suitable for youth and adults or as a home schooler's curriculum aid or a devotional guide for families. Church youth groups may use a free guide provided on the author's website to adapt the study guide to their needs. (*incorporates YouTube, virtual tours, satellite maps, and more.)

Kacey's Question: "Who Will I Marry?" (2018) is a picture book with a pop-up for young children, illustrated by Barbara Jones. As five-year-olds play dress-up on a rainy day or spend a day on the beach, each brings the question to storybook form. The question was asked by the author's daughter when she was five. Strangely enough, her daughter's son asked the same question twenty-five years later.

Contents

Chapter Titles and Scripture References

(Italics are quotes from the New International Version)

Prologue: Amorite Attack at Daybreak
Day 1 (Monday)
"Now Adoni-Zedek king of Jerusalem heard …
Gibeon had made a treaty of peace with Israel. …
Gibeon was an important city … and all its men were good fighters.
So Adoni-Zedek … appealed …
'Come up and help me attack Gibeon.' …
[And they] *took up positions against Gibeon and attacked it."*
Joshua 10:1-5
Page 29

Chapter 1: The Longest Day … Ever
Day 1 (Monday)
"The Lord threw them into confusion …
Israel pursued them along the road going up to Beth Horon …
the Lord hurled large hailstones down on them from the sky …
The sun stopped in the middle of the sky
and delayed going down about a full day …
a day when the Lord listened to a man." Joshua 10:10-14
Page 33

Final Words

"Judah could not dislodge the Jebusites ... in Jerusalem ..."
JOSHUA 15:63
*"The Benjamites ... failed to dislodge the Jebusites,
who were living in Jerusalem."* JUDGES 1:21
Page 243

Acknowledgements

Dr. Charles C. Ryrie and his *Ryrie Study Bible, Expanded Edition, NIV,* The Moody Bible Institute, 1994. Thank you for Dr. Ryrie and his encouragement of my project, which was a result of his chronological plan, "Read Through the Bible in a Year." His words to me, as I actively encouraged others to read God's word, "If they will only read it!"

Santa Claus, who took my request for a new Bible for Christmas and purchased Dr. Ryrie's "Expanded Edition," with the chronological reading plan in the front.

Caitlin Consolver, my granddaughter, whose enthusiasm for reading inspired her, at seven years of age, to want to write stories. Her words challenged me to take up a latent, life-long desire of my own.

My bulldog husband, George Consolver, who heard me when I said in 2009, "If I really write this, maybe I should go there." He found Associates for Biblical Research (ABR) and their archaeological dig at Khirbet el Maqatir, near Gibeon in the Palestinian West Bank.

Our heavenly Father, who surely superintended every aspect of that trip in 2010—from our Israeli tour guides with ABR to our beginning acquaintance and friendship with ABR staff, our personal Palestinian guide for our side trip to Gibeon, and much more.

Our ongoing relationship with Larry Carpenter of Carpenter Son's Publishing and with the graphic artist extraordinaire, Suzanne Lawing.

Yaron Sachs, our personal tour guide in 2017, who drove us all around the outskirts of old Jerusalem: the Waters of Nephtoah, the bin-Hinnom wadi, the Hill of Evil Council, the backside of the Mount of Olives, the wadi Joz, the mountain of Michmash, and more.

Character Names

ADONI-ZEDEK, King of Jerusalem. Joshua 10:1, 5.

AGH-TAAN, landowner at ein-el-Beled, the spring of Gibeon.

AMNED, Asherite, Hebrew leader of supply train carrying goods to and for Joshua's army. Numbers 2:27.

CRABAW, deserter from Zedek's army.

DAGAN, neglected son of the thief, big for his age, fifteen years old.

DANYA, wife of Ishtaba, mother of Eskie and Keshub.

DEYAB, old Bedouin who lives near Jericho's spring.

DUBO, from Beeroth, Joshua 9:17, one of the spies of Aijalon valley in Shepherd, Potter, Spy—and the Star Namer (SPSSN).

ESKIE, Gibeonite, seventeen years old, third son of Ishtaba, master potter of the Ra-eef' potters. Eskie is a hunter and a top student of the Hittite soldier's daily military training sessions on the summit of Gibeon.

GADITES, a Hebrew tribe tasked by Moses to lead the Hebrew army into battle. Numbers 32: 16-24, I Chronicles 12:8.

GHALEB, Sir, old Hittite soldier who trains young men of Gibeon every day to defend their homeland in Aijalon Valley. Joshua 10:2.

ISHTABA, called Baba by Eskie and Keshub, a Hivite and master potter of Gibeon. Leader of Gibeonite delegation that approached Joshua and asked for a treaty.

JALIL, 'Zalef's cousin, who will escort her to Gibeon.

JEBUS, expert archer and a Jebusite, forced into Zedek's Amorite army, son of Mahnon the master bowmaker held hostage in Zedek's palace dungeon in Jerusalem.

JOZMAN, a Jebusite and an uncle to Za'atar, Naqib, and Jebus's father Mahnon. "Inside man" living in Jerusalem for many years. In charge of all Zedek's building and city maintenance.

KESHUB, fifth son of master potter. Main character of SPSSN. Thirteen years old. Personal servant of Joshua.

LA-ANA, Eskie's sister, Ya-yah's wife.

LEHAB, Eskie's and Keshub's cousin. Lives in Ra-eef' courtyard, same age as Keshub.

MAK, a donkey taken as spoils of war at Makkedah.

MAKI THE GADITE, a young runner in Joshua's army.

MANDO, nine-year-old grandson of Zedek, dung carrier for the palace.

MAHNON, Jebus's father, the bow maker in Zedek's dungeon.

MATTAH, younger brother of cousin Lehab from SPSSN. Lives in Ra-eef' courtyard.

MOLECH, the god of the Amorites, who required the sacrifice of children in the fire.

NAQIB, Jebus's uncle, who lives in the valley of the craftsmen along the wadi-Joz. Expert arrow smith.

OCRAN, Naphtalite, Hebrew leader of the battlefield cleanup team. Numbers 2:29.

PHINEHAS, son of the high priest of the Hebrews. Numbers 25:7.

RACHEL, Ranine's wife.

RA-EEF', father of Ishtaba and his brothers, founder of Ra-eef' pottery.

RAGAR, shackled thief of Gibeon. Sentenced to one year in shackles, serving Gibeonite community.

RAJA, favorite donkey.

RAMATH, Moabite, camp cook for the woodcutters, supplying the Hebrews' tabernacle.

RAMI', fourth son of Ishtaba.

RANINE, Eskie's oldest brother, first son of Ishtaba.

'RAUNAH, an elder of the Jebusites, who farms the top of Mt. Moriah and has a threshing floor there, c.p. II Samuel 24:18-24.

RANGON, liveryman of Jerusalem, friend of Uncle Yaakoub.

RANGO, crippled son of Rangon. Sent home from Zedek's army with a broken leg. Cannot walk.

REEF, a giant of the Rephaim. Works for Za'atar. Lives in the rugged valley near the spring of Nephtoah. Deuteronomy 2:10-11.

SAMIR, UNCLE, younger brother of the master potter, operations and supply manager of Ra-eef' pottery business, an inventor. Eskie's mentor.

SAN-BAR, deaf sandal maker from Jebus's unit of Zedek's army.

XANDER, a younger Jebusite cousin to Jebus.

YAAKOUB, UNCLE, Ishtaba's brother; he took Ra-eef' pottery to market before he was injured.

YA-YAH', Eskie's brother-in-law, taking the place of Yaakoub as marketer of Ra-eef' pottery since Yaakoub's knee injury, while fleeing the Amorites.

'ZALEF, (Pickle Girl) cousin to Jebus; she lives at the spring of Nephtoah. She is named after the caper bush that appears to grow out of stones and that beautiful, delicate-appearing flowers, purplish stems, and thorns. 'Zalef the person exhibits many of the same qualities as her namesake. The wildflower's tightly closed green buds can be pickled in vinegar. It is tasty with gamey meats.

ZA'ATAR, father of 'Zalef; he produces wooden staves for making bows and arrows.

ZOBAR, Zedek's second son, in charge of Jerusalem when his father was executed at Makkedah by Joshua.

Foreword

The horde of Abraham's descendants had completed forty years wandering in the wilderness of the Sinai Desert. With supernatural backing, they entered the land of Canaan dominated by Amorite city-states. All but one vowed to defend Canaan at any cost.

Only four towns of Aijalon Valley in central Canaan took a different course of action. Led by a Hivite of Gibeon, they approached the Hebrews and asked for a treaty. For this, it is recorded:

"Now

Adoni-Zedek

King of Jerusalem …

Then the five kings of the Amorites—

The kings of Jerusalem,

Hebron, Jarmuth, Lachish and Eglon

Joined forces …

Against Gibeon

And attacked it."

JOSHUA 10:1, 5

"[And they]... *took up positions against Gibeon and attacked it.*"
JOSHUA 10:5

Prologue

On the ridge above Aijalon Valley at daybreak   *Day 1*

Full moon has set.

Gray light. Shadowy figures. The sizzle of glowing coals, doused. Wood smoke. Low voices. ... Tremulous voices. The scraping of whetstone with bronze. Fragrance of rosemary tea. Acute body odors.

A guttural challenge. ... A whimper of submission.

Jebus leaned his elbows on his knees and spat on his whetstone. The stone darkened. He palmed a cold metal haft. Circular movement calmed the fluttering in his stomach. He glanced at the horizon—lighter, not so gray.

"Wake them all," he spoke to his second. *If any can sleep.*

Shuffling feet. Rustling of bedrolls. Clank of gear.

"That is mine!"

"Are you sure?"

"This dagger says it is."

"Save it for the enemy, man."

"Humpf."

Jebus tucked his whetstone in his girdle and sheathed his short sword. "Pass it along. 'Gird up your loins.'"

Low murmurings. …

Shiz-z-z-z. Water meeting heat. Water wins. … *Strange thought.*

Glancing at the horizon. Brightening more. Light overcoming darkness. Another day arriving. A day to live? A day to die?

Fires blinking out on Gibeon's hill. Farmers and shepherds and potters. Good people. Solid people. Trained by the Hittite soldier. Defending their homes to the death.

A golden glow at the horizon beyond Gibeon's hill. *It is time.*

"Be ready, men, when the sun breaks the horizon. Pass it along." He shrugged his leather quiver over his shoulder and grabbed his bow, strung tight. He caressed the smoothness of the layered wood, sinew, and horn—feeling his father's strength. The bowmaker. In Zedek's dungeon.

No more thinking … just doing. This is for you, Baba.

The fiery rim of intense golden rays pierced the gloom and vanquished light's enemy.

Jebus thrust his fist high and sprang to action. "*Hi-ee-yah! Charge!*"

Down the rocky hillside. Swerving past large boulders. Leaping across shallow, dry water courses. Thunder of sandaled feet behind him. Curses of false courage.

Brandishing his sword. Legs churning. Leaning into the sprint to attack. Crossing a wheat field, newly harvested. Spikes of wheat straw piercing the tie-ons of his footwear. Irritation—barely registering.

The *whis-sk-t* of an arrow. A scream of surprise. His second crumpled in his side vision.

A flash of sunlight on oiled bronze. Lion faces. Grim counterattackers from the shadows. *Who are these men? Not Gibeonites! … Hebrews?*

Forward still. Running, feinting right. Ducking under a side-slash. Threshing floor in sight. *Reach Gibeonite men of reason. Call a truce! Negotiate for peace.*

In the shadow of Gibeon's hill. Hand to hand all around. Clashing of metal on metal. Click-clacking of spears.

Whack! "Wh-a-a?" ... Searing pain. Darkness.

Quiet.

"The Lord threw them into confusion ... Israel pursued them along the road going up to Beth Horon ... the Lord hurled large hailstones down on them from the sky ... The sun stopped in the middle of the sky and delayed going down about a full day ... a day when the Lord listened to a man." JOSHUA 10:10-14

Chapter 1
The Longest Day ... Ever

Aijalon Valley in Canaan   *Day 1*

Eskie meandered through the wheat field harvested only yesterday. While the enemy grew in numbers on the surrounding ridges, Gibeonite farmers wielded their scythes in panic. None of them knew if they would survive to eat the grain or not. Today, enemy Amorite soldiers lie strewn with the stubble.

Eskie bent to claim a crude bronze sword. He pried away the fingers of another raggedy soldier in the army of the fierce Adoni Zedek. The Amorite king of Jerusalem now ran for his life.

"Es-s-s-kie."

He straightened and surveyed the field around him. One alive among the slain who knew his name? He scratched the back of his head. Whom did he know among Zedek's soldiers? He had seen plenty of them over the last several moons. Their comings and goings above the wadi Qelt to spy on the Hebrews were as regular and routine as his own. But ... who? "Jebus! Where are you?"

"Un-n-n-h."

Eskie pivoted toward the sound, dropping his collection of bronze swords at his feet. Yes, a fist nearby clenched and unclenched in pain. A bow curved across the wounded man's back. An empty quiver confirmed the friend he spied with on Mt. Nebo—the expert marksman of Jerusalem.

Eskie knelt beside Zedek's reluctant soldier, unclasped the quiver, and turned his friend over with care. He poured a few dribbles from his pottery flask to moisten the archer's dried, cracked lips. Soaking the tail of his girdle, he dabbed at a goose egg on the side of his friend's head. Jebus gasped and became limp.

Eskie examined him for broken bones and glanced up for help. In the distance toward the Pass of Beth Horon, his little brother jogged down the trail. He last saw Keshub travelling beside Joshua, with Hebrew soldiers going over the pass at midday. They chased after the fleeing Amorites. "Keshub! Over here! I need help."

His little brother broke into a trot, leaping over downed soldiers. A bronze sword in its scabbard bobbed and jolted at his side. "Eskie! Have you noticed the sun has stopped moving? Joshua prayed to the One Most High and asked for the sun to stand still. The sun has stayed in place ever since!"

Eskie darted his gaze to the shadow at his feet, raising a single eyebrow. He had gathered three bundles of bronze swords from the battlefield since noon. The sun *should* be halfway down to the horizon by now. *What could this mean?*

Little brother flung his arms wide. "Eskie, the one who named the stars is the creator God of the Hebrews!"

"What?" Eskie shook his head. He had no time now for wild tales from his little brother. "Help me with Jebus. Remember our friend from Jerusalem?"

"Sure. Is he alive?"

Eskie knelt beside the archer of Jerusalem. "Alive, but badly injured. He is unconscious now, though he called my name earlier. Help me get him to the courtyard."

* * *

Eskie shifted Jebus's arm across his shoulders and sucked in a breath. "Hold on a little longer, man."¬¬ Gritting his teeth for one last effort, he climbed the few steps to the courtyard door.

Little brother, with the archer's bow and quiver over his shoulder, held the door open.

Surprised again to see his home littered with injured men, Eskie nodded a greeting. He headed for a shaded space at the wall next to his uncle.

With the sun high in the sky, Uncle Yaakoub sprawled on his pallet ... a rare sight among adults of the Ra-eef' family. He stopped his whittling and moved a stem of rosemary to the corner of his mouth. "Eskie, who do you have there?"

"One of Zedek's men. Kesh, give me a hand to ease him down."

"On-n-nh!" Jebus voiced his pain and roused.

Eskie knelt and pressed his water jug to his friend's lips.

"Eskie, we do not have space enough here for Amorites." Mamaa's nose flared, as she appeared, holding a small pottery bowl filled with steaming broth.

Eskie's stomach rumbled at the aroma. "His name is Jebus, Mamaa. He is not like the others."

Uncle Yaakoub looked up. "Danya, your boy is right. This young man is the son of the master bowmaker of Jerusalem."

Eskie rose and facing his mother. Her arched brow showed the disdain she felt for aiding one of the enemy. "Mamaa, this is the man I spied with from Mt. Nebo on the day I heard Moses say good-bye to Joshua."

Keshub nodded. "And he helped me on the night I kept watch alone at the turnoff from the el Gayeh trail."

"Still, with so many in need," Mamaa shook her head. "And your gran-mamaa probably drawing her last breath today ... I do not have time to take care of an Amorite, too."

"Madame, ... I never ... wanted to be counted as an Amorite. I am Jebusite. I was forced to serve the despicable Adoni-Zedek. Even now, my father is hostage in the king's dungeon. He would have been killed before my eyes if I had not joined the Amorites. ... I would not keep you from helping your own people."

Mamaa swiped the back of her hand across her brow, as she turned away. "Son, you must care for your friend until someone else is available. I must be with your gran-mamaa. This broth is for her, if she will eat it. And we are running low on supplies, as well as space. What I really need from you, Eskie, is to bring us a fat goose or two ... or an ibex."

Keshub spoke up. "Mamaa, may I sit with Gran-mamaa for a while? I want to tell her what happened today at Beth Horon pass, when Joshua prayed for the sun to stand still."

Mamaa turned back, dipped her chin, and frowned. "Wh-what?"

"I will explain." Little brother followed Mamaa into their home hewn into the hillside of solid limestone.

"Kesh and that crazy idea of his." Fists on his hips, Eskie muttered to himself and stepped into the sunshine. Still, his shadow lay close to his feet.

Uncle Yaakoub lifted his injured knee and grimaced. He waved Eskie toward the courtyard door. "Get us an ibex, Eskie. I can watch over our friend. If anything can heal a man from a head injury like that, the smell of roasting goat should. The thought of it melting in my mouth makes my knee feel better already. And since you are going that way, the men at the wood camp need supplies. Your Aunt Raga will make a pack for you before you leave. You can take a donkey."

* * *

"Raja, old girl, *what is happening*?" Climbing the steep path beside his donkey, Eskie removed his head wrap and tucked it in his girdle. "They should be well into second watch at the wood camp ... but the sun refuses to go down."

He combed his fingers through the mess of tangles and scratched his scalp, trying to stop the sounds of battle in his head. His shadow on the steep rise before him mimicked his frustration ... his elbow hacked at the line of trees beside the trail.

What did happen today? The sun ... stopped ... in the middle of the sky. At noon!

Raja swished her tail, her hooves clattering on the rocky path.

Keshub said Joshua prayed at noon. On Beth Horon Pass. Keshub, and now Baba, believe Joshua's god is that powerful. I do not know what to believe.

He forced one foot in front of the other on the rocky path. He spied on Joshua and his people for over three moons. Strange things happened before his eyes. One moment, the early morning sun glistened on the rushing waters of the Jordan River ... the next, the Hebrews crossed ... on dry ground.

And what about the fall of Jericho? Unbelievable. The strongest walls, the best fortified city of Canaan. But I saw ... those walls tumble outward. Joshua's army walked straight in. Burning Jericho lit my way home on that moonless night.

Eskie grasped a handful of Raja's mane to stop at a level place. He turned, resting his forearm on the donkey's warm flank and gazed down on Aijalon Valley, where the battle cleanup continued.

He pinched his nose to stifle the faint odor of burning flesh coming from below. *Will I ever get rid of the memory of Jericho?*

And now the battlefield in Aijalon Valley? "Raja, Gibeon was surrounded. I thought myself ready to fight to the death. We all would have died if Zedek had his way."

"What did our friend Jebus call his own king?" Eskie stroked Raja's curved hip. "Oh, yes, 'That oozing, pustulant boil of a man.' Words much too kind for the likes of Zedek. We worried about an invasion by the Hebrews who camped at Gilgal. But they just waited. I asked myself many times, while I spied on them from the perch, 'What ... are ... you ... waiting ... for?'"

Raja shook her head and snorted, shifting her stance.

Eskie rubbed his eyes with the heels of his hands. "Yes, you are right, Raja. It is time to go. We will get to the wood camp soon."

He stretched wide and yawned from the depth of his being. *The attack happened only this morning? Will this day never end?*

"Five kings ...[hid] in the cave at Makkedah. ... Joshua said, 'Open the ... cave. ... Do not be afraid. ... This is what the Lord will do to all [your] enemies.' ... [He] struck [them] ... and hung them on five trees. ...That day Joshua took Makkedah." JOSHUA 10:16-28

Chapter 2
The Flying Ibex

Sundown of the longest day ... ever   *Day 1*

At a rocky outcropping Eskie, glanced at the sun sinking into the Great Sea on the horizon. *Finally.* The promising fragrance of wood smoke tickled his nose.

Raja nodded her head and picked up her pace, pulling the lead rope through Eskie's hand.

"Whoa, girl. We are almost there. A little water and some grass will make it all worthwhile."

He placed two fingers in his mouth, *"Squee-ee-yew!"*

"Sque-e-et--yew-oo!" Ramath appeared at the top of the rise. "Eskie! Good to see you. We hoped someone would come tell us what happened. We watched the Hebrews go up the wadi Qelt last night. How is Gibeon?"

Eskie kissed one cheek, then the other cheek, of the camp cook. "Everything is good. I will tell you as soon as I unload my donkey.

Do you have water for her?"

"Of course. Dubo! Look who is here. Help him with his donkey, while I get Eskie some food."

With the evening star appearing, Eskie approached the fire. He nodded to Dubo across from him. "Old friend from the perch!"

The spy from Beeroth with the continuous black eyebrow ¬hunched forward with his hands on his knees. "You are here. That must mean good news in the valley. Hunh?"

Eskie darted his eyes to opposite sides of the fire, where Ragar and Dagan, shackled thief and neglected child, now a young man, avoided eye contact with each other.

Ragar, with one elbow resting on the upraised knee of his bronze-clad leg, removed a blade of grass he chewed and spat into the darkness. "What did the grand Ra-eefs do this time?"

Flumping his bedroll of homemade woolens to the ground, Eskie lowered his weary body and reached for the Ra-eef' pottery bowl the cook extended. Cook sank to his own bedroll next to him.

Eskie raked in a bite and washed it down with a swig from his water flask. "Men, our homes and our families survived."

Du-bo whistled his relief. "Tell us. How?"

Eskie set his bowl of lentil stew aside. "The invaders rescued us."

Dubo's eyebrow shot up.

Ramath slapped his thighs.

Ragar scowled.

Hands on his knees, elbows bent, Dagan leaned in. "How is that possible?"

Eskie took up a stick from the fire and scratched in the dirt. "As you saw, the Hebrews marched through the night last night in the wadi below. I was with them. Baba sent me early yesterday with a message from Gibeon, pleading for their help. Joshua's answer? His god had already told him to go to Gibeon. He said their god would give Gibeon's enemies into Joshua's hand. Joshua sent Keshub home to tell Baba the Hebrews would arrive by morning.

"Our men in Gibeon stayed ready all night with every weapon we had on the rocky ledges of Gibeon. The Amorites poured down at dawn, from their camps on the rim of the valley. But the Hebrew army flooded into the valley, with the rising sun behind them, stopping the attackers in their tracks."

He paused and searched the eyes of his listeners. "By noon, the valley was strewn with Zedek's men. What was left of them headed for the pass at Beth Horon, and Joshua's army chased after."

Staring into Ragar's angry countenance, he went on, "According to my little brother, who was with Joshua at Beth Horon, Joshua stopped at the pass. He decided they could not catch all the fleeing armies before the sun went down. So Joshua prayed ... to the God Most High ... to stop the sun from setting. He commanded his men to keep the run-away Amorites from reaching their walled cities."

The crackle of the fire filled the silence.

Cook added a piece of wood to the glowing coals. "And you believe that?"

"Ramath, I do not know what to believe. I know this afternoon was the longest in my life." He counted on his fingers. "I know I gathered three loads of weapons from the battlefield before Keshub arrived. I know we carried a wounded Jebusite to the courtyard. I walked all the way here from Gibeon ... and the sun has just now gone down. I know I am so tired I cannot eat, and that has never happened before in my life. ... You tell me what happened today."

Dagan picked up a pebble, hurled it at his father's midsection, and jeered. "Seems like I remember your big mouth saying you would believe what you heard about the Hebrews when the sun stood still. What does the big ... Amorite ... man ... think about the Hebrews now?" Red-faced, he spat into the fire, then gritted his teeth and glared at his father.

Ragar flinched, rubbed his stomach, and cast a sidewise glance at his offspring. "Hunh." He turned his back to his son and the fire and stretched out on his bedroll.

Eskie reached to comfort Dagan, as the young man leapt to his feet and plunged into the darkness of the forest.

* * *

At the wood camp   *Day 2*

Eskie awoke to an owl's soft who-hoot. The waning moon lit the wood camp, as he donned his girdle and tucked in the flat-bread from last night's uneaten meal inside. He added the belt and scabbard from the Amorite loot he found yesterday. *Was it just yesterday? The day I will never forget. Will I ever make sense of it?*

He geared up with the Ra-eef' pottery water flask, his quiver of arrows, and the trusted master-crafted bow made by Jebus's father. He paid a yearling lamb for it two harvests ago.

His stomach growled. Maybe he should eat the lentil stew Ramath offered last night. Cold, bland, nothing like Mamaa's. He shrugged. *Maybe it will keep my stomach quiet and not scare off the ibexes.*

He startled Dubo, keeping watch on a rock near the tethered donkeys. "Sorry, friend. I want to get to the spring before the ibex herds arrive at dawn. Cook could use some meat to flavor your lentil stew."

"Good hunting. I wish I were going with you."

"Thanks. Another day maybe."

"Yes. I would like that."

Down the path worn by the wood campers, Eskie found the faint ibex trail that headed into the underbrush. He retrieved a long stem of rosemary from his girdle. Rolling the piney-fragranced herb between his hands, he bruised the leaves to release the sticky oil. He rubbed it over his exposed skin. Mamaa swore his favorite herb for stews would scare away flying and crawling critters. He hoped the pungent smell would mask his own ripening scent.

He took each step with care through the dense growth of sumac brushing his shoulders. Its red berries appeared almost black in the moonlight. He would pick some on the way back to camp for the cook to use.

* * *

Eskie shifted the awkward bundle draped over his shoulder. Holding the doe ibex by her horns, he sucked in several deep breaths. One more push up the slope, and he would reach the wood camp. Too bad he did not find the herd of female ibexes earlier in the day. Now he had to spend another night here.

As he neared the camp, angry shouting broke the calm of the forest. Ten more paces, and he entered the clearing, as Dagan head-butted his father's midsection.

Ragar stepped back to keep his balance, his son's head still planted in his stomach. The prisoner wood chopper launched a left-handed uppercut to Dagan's chest. The blow sent the boy reeling backward, until he tripped over a stack of hewn logs. He fell hard.

Before Dagan regained his footing, Ragar picked up his ax and stepped toward his son.

With no time to think, Eskie planted his left foot and took hold of both horns of the young ibex. He twisted to his left and dipped his shoulder, as he took a power stride forward, and swung the carcass sidewise with all his might. The ibex flew the short distance between them and connected with Ragar's back ... knocking him flat on his face.

Wide-eyed and grasping his chest where he sprawled, Dagan wheezed air into his lungs. "He would have killed me." He hiccupped and covered his face with his forearm. His shoulders heaved, and great sobs escaped.

Eskie pulled the overgrown young man up and wrapped him in his arms.

Dagan shrugged off the embrace and bent at the waist, grasping his midsection.

Eskie nodded to the cook and pointed his chin at the wild goat across Ragar's downed body. "Please string up the fresh meat for the night, Ramath. I will be back."

Draping his arm across the young man's shoulders, he led the long-ago-rejected son away. At the rocky outcropping on the slope below, Eskie slumped beside his young friend … waiting … as the orange ball slid into the Great Sea.

Dagan huffed through clenched teeth, "Why does my father hate me?"

…

"There are many things I do not understand … Like why does the sun come up and go down again? … Day after day?"

"Then Joshua ... moved on ... to Libnah and attacked it.
The Lord also gave [Libnah] *and its king*
into Israel's hand." JOSHUA 10:29-30

Chapter 3
Dagan the Brave

At the wood camp   *Day 3*

"Eskie."

A nudge at his elbow. "Hunh?"

"Are you going to sleep all day?"

"What? Sleep all day?" He brought down the arm draped across his eyes. Bright light assaulted, turning the inside of his eyelids red. He darted his hand to his brow and opened his eyes a slit.

Ramath stood over him with a pottery bowl. "Do you want to drink this? Or should I pour it on you?" His sandaled foot nudged Eskie's shoulder. "You slept like a dead man. Missed the excitement at midnight. Slept right through it. You missed breakfast, too. The men are already working."

Eskie rubbed his eyes. Finally, he understood the throbbing in his head came with every blow of Ragar's ax splitting wood for the camp of the Hebrews. Eskie laid aside his homespun woolen blanket and rocked to a sitting position. "I will drink it. Thanks."

He gulped and squinted a glance at the sun … already nearing midmorning? "Oh, no! I must go home. Why did you not wake me sooner?" He gulped again from the rough pottery bowl.

Ramath motioned him to the fire circle.

Eskie thrust feet in his sandals and tied them on. This all started with the ruse of Baba and the delegation wearing worn-out sandals to meet the invading enemy. His own sandals would soon be fit for their disguise.

Ramath offered flatbread and a warm bowl of weak mutton broth and returned to his makeshift kitchen under an oak.

Eskie chuckled. "Ramath, did you hear about the stale, moldy bread that got us into this wood-camp situation?"

Ramath wrestled with a hindquarter of the ibex. "Yes, I heard. I also heard your mother was none too happy about sending bread not fit to eat. She was afraid it would ruin her reputation as a cook." He chuckled, too. "I understand what she meant. But if Balak, king of Moab, saw me serving moldy bread, it would cost me more than my reputation. The pompous old goat would have said 'off with his head!'"

"Did you say something about excitement at midnight? What happened?"

"Yes. Quite a rumpus you missed. Dagan and the donkeys heard it first … a lion roaring off yonder." Ramath waved his new bronze knife in the direction of Moab. "Surely the scent of the goat hanging in the tree drew him here. As he got closer, all of us were awake, and Dagan stood between the ibex's tree and the lion's roar."

"Brave lad."

Cook thrust a sturdy branch whittled smooth and sharp through the flesh. With muscles bulging, he lifted the ibex hind-quarter by both ends of the branch. He suspended it over the coals between two stumps with matching grooves.

He dipped his chin, staring straight into Eskie's eyes, then glanced Ragar's way across the clearing where he split logs. "The rest of us were struggling to get our sandals on, when we heard the lion yelp close by. All by himself, Dagan sent that lion running back to his den."

"That young man received slaps on the back for a job well done from Dubo and me. He did not look at his father, and Ragar did not get the chance to belittle the boy. I stood over him with my new bronze butcher's knife if he tried."

"Whoa! I slept through all that?"

"You did." Ramath lowered his voice. "And I am thinking, Eskie, you should take Dagan back with you. It is not good for him to be here with his father ... disrupts the whole camp. And, one day, they might kill each other."

"Yes, I know, but it will leave you short—"

"*Spre-ee-ah! ... Spre-ee-ah!*"

"Is that reinforcements?" Ramath cleaned his hands with a cloth hanging from his girdle.

Eskie jumped to his feet and charged to the head of the trail. "Na-gosh', old cousin. What brings you here at this time of day?"

"We came halfway yesterday and camped at the spring below. This is our new man from Kephirah. Did you hear a lion last night?"

Ramath hee-hawed like a donkey. "The rest of us did, but Eskie slept through it all. Must have been the flying ibex that took his strength away. Heh, heh."

Na-gosh' grimaced. "A flying ibex?"

Eskie took a lead rope from his father's cousin and led the animal to the camp kitchen. "Save it for the campfire, Ramath, after I am gone. Let's get these fellows settled in. Now both Dubo and Dagan can return to Gibeon with me."

◌◑◐◍

Returning to the Hebrew camp

Keshub turned up his Ra-eef' water flask, made by his father's own hands. He palmed its grainy surface and gulped. Gazing back to where he grew up as fifth son of the master potter, he wiped his mouth and smiled, tears clouding his eyes.

Gran-mamaa and Baba had carried the weight of an ancient curse of slavery on their family for many years. He knelt with his father beside Gran-mamaa two nights ago, as her breathing grew weaker. He told her stories master Joshua told him about his God, and she breathed deeper for a moment, then smiled.

Finally, she whispered, "He *is* the One who knows *the heretofore and the hereafter*. Your gran-baba worried about the curse of slavery he learned about when his father died. All along … the Star Namer … meant the curse for our good."

Keshub turned again toward the blue hills of Moab and descended the familiar rocky trail toward Gilgal. A lump knotted in his throat at traces of a campfire halfway down the steep incline to the Jordan Valley. Baba explained to him the purpose of the strange delegation here. Dressed in raggedy clothing, hardly fit to wear, and sandals falling apart, he doubted his father's wisdom. Would they really meet the Hebrew horde like a defenseless flock of sheep … approaching a lion?

He told himself that day, "Trust Baba." But doubts kept coming.

Down the trail, Jericho came into view. Keshub shook his head at the blackened heap of what was left of the most powerful city of Canaan—and the most fortified. A year or so ago, he longed for adventures beyond Aijalon Valley. He pursed his lips. *I never wished to be a slave. If Baba had not asked for a treaty, I would not be a slave now.* But, without the treaty, all of Gibeon and the other cities of our valley would surely be destroyed. *And I would not have heard all the wonderful stories about Joshua's God.*

Baba was right. He knew the God of the Hebrews was different. Real. And powerful. Baba believed learning more about this Hebrew God was worth the risks.

Rounding the ruins of Jericho, Keshub knelt at the gushing

spring, his hands gripping the rocks that lined the pool. He slurped with gusto.

"Hal-low, lad. Gibeonite, right?"

"Yessir. Keshub."

"Ah, yes. You survived the Hebrews' attack on Gibeon? What happened?"

"It was the Amorites who attacked Gibeon. Joshua's army came to defend Aijalon Valley against Zedek and the others. The Hebrews saved Gibeon."

The old gentleman hobbled nearer. "Did I hear you right? I thought you said the enemy of Canaan saved you Gibeonites."

"Yes, sir. You heard right." Keshub shook his head and shrugged. "Did you notice the sun stood still for a long time on the day before yesterday?"

The toothless, old Bedouin, peered from watery eyes and dipped his chin. "I did notice. Why? I thought surely I imagined it."

"You did not imagine it. My master, Joshua, prayed at Beth Horon Pass and asked the God Most High of the Hebrews to stop the sun from going down. So he could catch all the fleeing Amorites."

Old Deyab's bushy, gray eyebrows arched high. "Is ... that ... right?"

CR80

Moon rising at Gibeon

Eskie hung the pack gear high on its peg in the stacked stone wall of the Ra-eef' livestock pen. "Men, you can wash up at the spring when you finish with the donkey. My mother will have something for us to eat in the courtyard. I will take her this ibex."

At the courtyard door, he adjusted the meaty burden on his shoulder before reaching for the leather handle. The gate flew open in his face, and he stepped back. A tousle-headed Ra-eef' young man with a yoke and two empty water jars burst out.

"Mattah! Thanks, man, for opening the gate for me and not running me down. You would not want our little ibex here to hit the ground."

Lehab's little brother stopped, startled. "Ibex? Did you get it with an arrow? On the first shot? Will you be here for the archery contest at the longest-day celebration? I saw you win it last year."

Eskie chuckled. "Slow down, Mattah. We can talk later. Get your mamaa water from the spring. We will need plenty of it, I am sure."

"Eskie!"

Baba's booming voice brought a quick lump to his throat. Since he crossed the Jordan River with Jebus three moons ago and spied on the Hebrew camp from Mt. Nebo, Baba called him only Eschol.

Big brother Ranine rose from the fire circle and helped Baba take the ibex from him, carrying it between them to the kitchen area.

Mamaa laid out her leatherwork cloth to receive the welcome addition to their food supply and hurried across the courtyard to clasp his roughened hands. "Eskie, I am so glad you are home." Grief etched her face. "Your gran-mamaa passed just before morning yesterday. Keshub was with her all that night." One hand went to her mouth. "He told her stories from Joshua about the God Most High of the Hebrews."

Baba returned to place his arm across Mamaa's shoulder and spoke in a low voice, "She is with Baba Ra-eef' now on the slope above the threshing floor."

Eskie drew in a deep breath, and his stomach clenched. More changes. *What could be next?*

"Then Joshua ... moved on from
Libnah to Lachish ..." JOSHUA 10:31

Chapter 4
Mission Salem

Late evening in the Ra-eef' courtyard   *Day 3*

Eskie turned the spit and rearranged glowing coals to direct heat onto the roasting ibex. Who could sleep anyway with the aroma filling his nostrils?

The injured expert archer of Jerusalem cleared his throat. "Eskie, I talked with your baba about this, and I have his permission to ask you to help me. I must return to Jerusalem as soon as possible. I am better, but I still feel dizzy when I first stand. I need you to go with me."

Uncle Yaakoub leaned in closer. "It will be dangerous, lad. We heard roving bandits lurking along the trail to Jerusalem. Probably Zedek's deserters. You have to be careful."

"And the situation may be more desperate in Jerusalem." Jebus drew in a deep breath. "Zedek's second son was left in charge when Zedek led his army to attack here. With the reckless son, Zobar, in charge, I expect nothing but bad news for my father. Zedek took him hostage to force me to stay in his army. He forced my father to make bows in his dungeon."

Jebus stared into the burning coals. "My father's life is in grave danger. Zobar is unpredictable on a good day. What must he be like when he is cornered like a young lion surrounded by a pack of wolves? I need to return to Jerusalem … now. I cannot wait another day. You must help me, please."

Uncle Yaakoub nodded. "Son, your father agrees you are the only one of us who can help Jebus return. But you cannot go alone. Too dangerous. If Dubo and Dagan are willing, we can send them with you. Dubo's mother has moved here to Gibeon and is living in Ragar's old house. She comes to help your mamaa every day in the courtyard. Tonight, your baba sent those young men to spend the night with her. As a widow in Beeroth, she and Dubo were always poor, but, without her son, she was destitute."

Uncle Yaakoub cleared his throat. "I have a friend in Jerusalem. The liveryman, Rangon, and his crippled son will help you, I am sure. Zedek forced the son into his army but sent him back with a broken leg and forever a cripple."

"We may need more than just the four of us, plus a liveryman and a crippled son." Eskie turned from the fire to Jebus.

"You will have plenty more. Most of my clan lives on the other side of Mt. Moriah. People call it the valley of the craftsmen. Not only are my uncles and cousins craftsmen, but they are also hunters and marksmen. We kept many of our men hidden when Zedek conscripted every young man in the area with hair on his lip."

Jebus lowered his eyes. "Still, three of our best did not escape Zedek's brutes. They were not in my unit. I do not know what happened to them in the battle." He cleared his throat. "We will go to the Spring of Nephtoah first. It is closer, and one of my uncles lives there."

Eskie yawned. "That is a plan to start with. We will see what Dubo and Dagan say in the morning. For now, I need sleep."

Uncle Yaakoub swatted a mosquito and turned the spit. "You

men sleep. I can tend to our flying ibex all night. Not sure I could sleep anyway with this smelling so good. Eskie, snap a few more rosemary stems from your gran-mamaa's bush yonder, and toss them around the edges of the fire. That should keep these pests away for a while."

* * *

On the trail to Jerusalem   *Day 4*

Eskie wished his head could do a complete swivel. Someone watched them. He sensed it. Perhaps because no birds sang from the rocky ridge above the narrow trail. *Could he count on Jebus on the other side of the donkey to help at all?* Jebus needed the donkey to steady him just to walk.

Eskie knew the trail to Jerusalem, but not like his little brother Keshub, who went to market with Uncle Yaakoub … in the old days. Hunh. Old days being a little more than two moons ago … before Jericho fell and burned.

His ears prickled. He whispered over his shoulder, "Jebus … How are you feeling?"

"A little wobbly. But your donkey helps much," he whispered, too.

Up ahead, Dubo seemed alert. *If we only knew what to expect. But what happens next, or the hereafter according to Baba, and Keshub is known only to—*

"Stawb in your tragh, man!" A rough hand grabbed Eskie's arm. A knifepoint pricked his left side.

Eskie sucked in a breath.

"Whack." The attacker slumped to the ground.

Eskie turned. "What was that?"

"I carried a stone … just in case,"

The ambusher squirmed at his feet.

Jebus rounded the donkey's backside, wearing a quizzical expression. "Sanbar?"

"You know this man?"

"Yes, he was in my unit." Jebus crouched beside the downed attacker, steadying himself with Uncle Samir's crutch and reaching to turn the man over.

Their marauder resisted and curled into a tight ball. "Don' hurh me."

"'Don't hurt me?'" Eskie placed his fists at his hips. "What kind of unit did you have?"

"Not a great one. This man is deaf."

"Deaf?" Eskie checked on Dubo up ahead, still keeping watch around them for other desperadoes. "Hunh." He bent down to help the trembling man. Perhaps if a deaf man would see Jebus, he would cooperate. Then they could get out of this very dangerous situation … stopped on the trail at a natural ambush point. *Yeah. Why did I not see him come from the left?*

Always dependable Dubo followed orders to stay alert in the lead, no matter what, and Dagan, in the rear, had not shown himself. *I hope he is all right.*

Jebus grasped the man's chin with his left hand and gave him a soft slap.

Tight-shut eyes flew open. In a moment, he focused on the friendly face backlit by sunlight.

"Sanbar, let me help you up." Jebus offered his hand.

The unlikely soldier unfolded and stood. "Mr. Je-buh?"

"Yes, man." Jebus offered him his new Ra-eef' water flask. The ambusher grabbed it and gulped. Jebus hastened to retrieve it, nodding at Sanbar and pointing to the ground. "Do not forget your awl."

"He was going to stab me with an awl?" Eskie pushed his hair off his forehead.

"Yes. He is a sandal maker by trade … from Moab."

"Great. Now we have a cripple, a dimwit, a pup, and a deaf sandal maker with an awl in our unit. Uncle Yaakoub will love telling this story. I hope we live through it."

* * *

Eskie secured the sandal maker's head wrap and tested how sturdily the rosemary bush's roots clung to the next rocky ledge. Several small branches had been snapped from the bush recently. If he could find where the men had camped, perhaps he could determine how many he had to … take out.

A pebble hit him on the shoulder. "Up here!" Dagan's hoarse whisper directed him.

Eskie hoisted himself to his young friend's level, where Dagan had pointed. "Looks like three of them slept here. The ashes are warm."

"Yes. By the depth of the ashes, they were probably here for two or three days—most likely since they deserted Zedek's army. I do not see evidence of food. These men will be desperate to attack us for the vittles we carry."

"What can we do?" Dagan's left hand rested on the bronze sword now tucked in his girdle, his right hand pressed to his midsection.

"I changed head wraps with our new friend. You saw?"

"Yes, why?"

"Sanbar is his name. Jebus knows him. Says he is a dependable chap, even if he is not so brave … from Jebus's unit of Zedek's army. And he is deaf."

"Deaf?"

"Yes. Now he is beside the donkey in my place, but I am hoping these ambushers will not suspect he is not me. You stay behind our men and the donkey, above them and out of sight. Keeping watch just like we said before, with your slingshot ready if they need your help. I plan to catch up with these fellows without their knowing and attack them before they ambush us. Understand?"

"Yes."

"Then Joshua ... moved on from Libnah
[and arrived at] *Lachish ...."* JOSHUA 10:31

Chapter 5
Ambush

On the trail to Jerusalem Day 4

Eskie rounded the hilltop, keeping a low profile. He flattened himself behind a boulder the length of a three-camel caravan and out of sight of the three men below. The ambushers lay flat on a ledge directly over the trail. He scratched at his temple, hoping the borrowed head wrap did not harbor lice.

He palmed a fist-sized stone and lobbed it to hit ground a few paces back ... on the other end of the boulder, providing refuge. The rock clattered and skipped down the hillside.

All three Amorite deserters below bobbed their heads and turned toward the sound. Ruffian number one shoved the young boy beside him and nodded toward the place from where the falling rock had come. The youth protested, but big, brave man pulled a bronze sword from his belt, threatening to use it on the kid.

Younger than Keshub and too young for army duty, the unlikely ambusher climbed toward the stone's launching point.

Eskie removed Sanbar's head wrap and unwound it. Good, no

visible lice. Encouraging. He crept nearer to where the lad would emerge, keeping flat against the limestone. He stopped at a small cleft.

The sound of footsteps approached the opening, then slowed.

Good. You should be cautious. Eskie took slow, silent, open-mouthed breaths.

Another step. The unwilling attacker stopped.

One more, young fellow. You are almost here. We will be better company than what you have now.

The undersized youth half-emerged into the opening, weapon-less.

Eskie flattened himself more and held his breath.

The lad looked to his right first.

Eskie pounced on him, head wrap in both hands, and clapped the cloth to the boy's mouth, drawing him back against his own chest. He whispered between clenched teeth, "Quiet! Do not struggle. You will be better off with us than the rascal you are with."

The trembling ambusher relaxed a bit.

Eskie kept a firm hold. "You were in Zedek's army?"

He nodded once.

"Did you know Jebus? He is my friend, and he is with me."

The youth completely relaxed against Eskie and shook his head yes.

"If I remove this gag, will you keep quiet?"

Vigorous nodding.

Eskie gathered the two ends of the cloth in one hand and tightened his grasp, drawing his weapon from his girdle. "If you cry out, I will have to use my dagger on you."

Zedek's young soldier trembled, nodding. Eskie let go and backed him into the cleft, pointing at the ground with his knife.

Subdued, the young man dropped down. Eskie handed him his water juglet and whispered, "Just a little." And took it back. "Stay here."

He slipped behind a nearby juniper tree and waited for the second ambusher to emerge from the place where he had first observed the three men below ... well, two men and a boy.

Through the fringe of juniper leaves, surprise registered on the face of a young man who appeared with bow drawn and arrow inserted. He lowered his bow ever so little when he saw his friend sitting still. "Wha-?"

The lad whispered and motioned. "Come over here and get down! Jebus is with him!"

Dubo and the others would be rounding the bend of the trail below at any moment. Eskie had no time to spare. He stepped from behind the juniper on the run, sheathing his bronze dagger, and rasped. "Jebus is coming now. I will take out the other one and explain later."

Eskie grabbed a sling stone almost the size of his fist from his shoulder bag, placing it in his sling at the ready. He stepped from behind the sheltering rock to see Jebus and Sanbar only a little way up the trail. Ruffian number one brandished his sword and positioned himself to attack.

Eskie sent his sling stone to whirring overhead and held his breath at the release. "Whack." The rounded stone found its mark. The Amorite deserter caught it in the back of his head. He splayed his arms wide, releasing his weapon. The bronze sword split the silence, as it clattered onto the trail below.

Eskie's heart rose to his throat. *Where is Dubo?*

* * *

Eskie leaned against a limestone backrest watching over the trail. He counted on his fingers, assessing his attack force. Jebus, the expert archer with a head wound—who sees double. Dubo, the strong, dependable, and loyal friend from the spies' nest over Gilgal, now brandishing the ambusher's long sword that fell at his feet. Dagan, the rejected son of the thief of Gibeon, who does not know his own worth. San-bar. *What are the strengths of a stuttering sandal maker who is deaf?* And, now, these two half-starved waifs from Zedek's army.

Jebus stirred the small fire, heating water in a Ra-eef' cookpot. He lowered his chin and pointed the glowing end of his stick at the younger of two new recruits. "How did you join up with that coward, Crabaw, son?"

The lad swallowed his morsel of dried fig with a gulp. "Sir, I tripped when a rock moved under my foot on the rush down the rim of Aijalon Valley. Crabaw pretended to care and stopped to help me up, never taking his eyes off our unit commander, rushing into battle ahead of us. Then he grabbed my arm and dragged me aside to hide, until all our unit engaged in hand-to-hand combat below us."

"Then what?" Jebus kept his piercing black eyes on the youth, demanding the truth.

The boy's gaze never wavered. "He found out I am a grandson of Zedek and would not let me out of his sight. He intended to use me as his excuse to return to Jerusalem as a hero." The product of a son of Zedek gave a rueful smile. "Crabaw did not know I am merely the offcast of a disfavored son. I carried water to the dungeon and took dung out for the last two years."

Eskie removed the blade of grass from his mouth. "Is that right? You know the palace well?"

"Like the back of my hand, sir. My name is Mando."

Jebus raised his chin and glanced Eskie's way. Their eyes locked for a moment.

Jebus directed his glowing stick and harshest stare at the second ambusher. "Xander, how did you join up with Crabaw?"

Eskie arched his eyebrows, and his mouth curved down. *How did Jebus know this young man?*

Xander squirmed and hung his head. "Sir, the day before the

battle, I must have eaten some bad meat. I was running into the woods at all hours of the night and day. When I missed the charge down the hillside and was confronted by Crabaw, I did not know what else to do. With the battle obviously going so badly down below, I could think of nothing else but going home to the crafts-men's valley."

Jebus eased a bit. "You are not the first of Zedek's army to be defeated by his meager provisions. Your baba and mamaa will be glad to see you return. How are you feeling now?"

"Better. Starving. That mutton broth smells good."

"Almost ready."

* * *

Eskie's stomach growled. They shared their own short rations to feed the starved, young men, before they collapsed. Alone now and keeping watch high above the others, he stifled a laugh. What a great gift of the hapless, young soldier and cousin to Jebus and the young one who knew the recesses of Zedek's palace and prison. *Gift? A gift implies a giver, Eschol … like the star's name implies* a star namer.

Eskie angled his chin skyward. Today, the sun followed its usual arc toward the Great Sea. No more stopping in its path. Shadows stretched longer at their normal rate. Anyone could tell the time of day by the shadow at their feet. Since the age of seven harvests, he knew this. How could everything be different on one day, three days ago? *Keshub … said the god of the Hebrews stopped the sun … because Joshua prayed.*

Eskie shook his head to clear his thinking. No time for that now. Almost ambushed twice already, if they were to get to the waters of Nephtoah tonight, they must go now. He whistled. *"Squee-ee-yew!"*

He washed down the last bite of dried fig with one swallow of his diminishing water supply. "I hope you can make it to Nephtoah, Jebus. We need you. *I need you. And we all could use some help from above. ... If there is such a thing. ... Dubo's new sword came from above.*"

"[Joshua and all his army] *took up positions against* [Lachish] ..."
JOSHUA 10:31

Chapter 6
Pickle Girl

Near Jerusalem at the
Waters of Nephtoah

Day 4,
continuing

On the crest above the waters of Nephtoah, Eskie mopped his brow with the tail of his girdle. Just as Jebus described it, a peaceful scene lay below. A small, tree-covered pond of spring-fed water, with a stone house and a grape arbor. Jebus's wistful tale of reaching his uncle's home and safety seemed within reach.

Eskie tilted his head back. The backdrop of the peaceful scene slanted up a steep, rocky mountain. Jebus said some folks called it the hill of evil counsel. From there, he would spy out Jerusalem on the other side and plan their moves to rescue Jebus's father in Zedek's dungeon.

An older woman tended a cook fire on the east side of the house in deepening shade. A young woman emerged with a water jar from the door facing him. He pressed himself deeper into shadow, as she scanned in his direction.

"That must be 'Zalef." Eskie chuckled at Jebus's cousin's name.

A girl named for a thorny pickle bush. Mamaa gathered its green buds and soaked them in saltwater and wine vinegar. Even now, Uncle Yaakoub might be eating slow-roasted ibex and popping capers in to help the gamey flavor.

His mouth watered at the thought of food, as the girl walked barefoot on the path to the water hole and disappeared behind tall reeds.

He placed both hands beside his shoulders to push up.

A blood-curdling scream split the peaceful calm. He leapt to his feet, staying low, and loped toward Nephtoah, swiveling his head left and right.

Unsheathing his bronze dagger, he crept through the rushes. Perhaps a snake frightened her on her path to water. He first spied 'Zalef's water pot lying smashed against a rock. Turning his head to a muffled sound, he spied a snake of a different kind.

One massive, grubby hand clamped over her mouth and pressed her to his chest, while the other lifted her off the ground and clasped her at the waist. She twisted and turned, kicking with savage power at her attacker's knees, while her hands clawed at his arms.

Before the oaf could notice his presence, Eskie slithered through the boggy growth and yanked one beefy ankle to make him fall flat on his back. The air wheezed out of his lungs on impact, and he lost his grip on his quarry.

Eskie leapt to his feet, brandishing his dagger, and crouched, scanning for other attackers in the undergrowth.

"Relax, hero. There is only one. At least only one at a time." Her voice dripped with sarcasm, as she scrambled to her feet, smoothing her head covering. "Who are you? And where did you come from?"

Who am I and where did I come from? ... What just happened here? Eskie shrugged. "Your attacker is reviving, should I tie him up?"

"Him? He is harmless."

"You know this oaf who just now assaulted you?"

"Of course. He is Reef. He lives in the next village that way." She pointed in the opposite direction of Jerusalem. "He did not look harmless a moment ago."

"Looks can be deceiving. He wants to marry me." She grimaced, one hand on her hip, her other pointed at him. "You, I do not know. Who are you and why are *you* here?"

He placed his hand on his heart and lowered his chin. "I am Eskie, third son of the master potter of Ra-eef' of Gibeon. Obviously, I came when I heard you scream. I thought you needed help. I am sorry I inconvenienced you and your beau here." Eskie reached a hand to the huge-fisted man to offer him help up.

"He is not my beau. And why were you lurking nearby?" Her lips tilted in a scowling challenge.

"I was not lurking. I was scouting for my band of men who will be arriving soon."

Pickle girl's scowl changed to pressed lips and lowered chin. "Why?"

"I believe, Pickle Girl, I am bringing your cousin Jebus home from the battle three days ago in Aijalon Valley."

She sucked in a breath and clapped a hand over her mouth. "Is Jebus all right?"

"No. He has a head injury and is barely able to walk. But he is better. He will need to rest here for a few days."

"And you have others with you? Who are they?"

"A small band with a mission to free Jebus's father from the dungeon of Zobar in Jerusalem."

"How many?"

"Seven, counting me."

Turning toward the rock house and stepping out, "Then I need to get supper started for the lot of you. You need to come get water jars and carry more water to the house."

Eskie's jaw dropped, as Pickle Girl disappeared from view, her golden head covering barely visible, bobbing through the tops of the reeds. "And do not call me Pickle Girl. My name is 'Zalef'."

Eskie turned and looked up to the big man still trying to draw a deep breath. "You are called Reef? Are you staying for supper, too?"

* * *

Under a starlit sky, Eskie reached to the center of the dinner mat to mop up the last bit of lentil stew still clinging to the large pottery bowl. He chewed the last morsel of flat bread, wanting to ask who made the stew. *If it was Pickle Girl, she is a good cook. Almost as good as Mamaa.*

Jebus stretched and yawned. "Eskie, Jerusalem is just over the steep rise here. I suggest you and Mando climb to the top tomorrow and observe the Amorite stronghold from afar. Xander and I need time to recuperate. Perhaps a day of rest will do your men some good, as well, while you devise a plan. Agreed?"

"Sure."

Dubo slung his bedroll and knapsack over his shoulder. "Sounds good to me."

Dagan groaned like an old man, as he rose and followed Dubo to the roof of the stone house.

Eskie stroked the short stubble at his chin. "Say, what did your cousin mean when she said, 'There is only one at a time.'?"

"By the full moon Reef and his two brothers switch off working for us. They are strong woodsmen who help us fell oaks and bring them here to prepare the wood for making bows. All three have sworn their love for 'Zalef, but she refuses them all. The old lady is a neighbor who comes to stay while my uncle is away."

Eskie swallowed the last of his rosemary tea and turned to his bedroll near the fire circle on the sunup side of the rock house. "I would like to get a couple of ducks from the pond before I leave tomorrow. Perhaps we can have roasted duck tomorrow evening."

Jebus raised his eyebrows. "Go to the far end of the pool if you do. 'Zalef is famous in the family for her pickled duck eggs. She would not be happy if you scattered her pet flock near the spring."

Eskie chuckled. "I see. We certainly want to keep 'Zalef happy. I am already of questionable value since I saved her from the gentle giant snoring over there."

CRSO

At the Hebrew camp at Gilgal.   *Day 4*

Outside Joshua's tent, Keshub swiped at the reed mat with his broom. With Joshua on the battlefield, he had no fire to build here, no rosemary tea to make, no messages to deliver. He shaded his eyes and gazed homeward to the ridge above Jericho. Questions chased one after another between his ears. *What is happening in Aijalon Valley with my family? With Joshua beyond Beth Horon Pass?*

Arriving in Gilgal yesterday, he searched through Joshua's things in his tent. He packed up anything he found that his master might need. Things Joshua might have forgotten, as he readied his army to attack the Amorites. *I will be ready if Joshua sends for me.*

"Young man!"

Keshub startled and whirled around, knocking into the tripod washstand that held mamaa's favorite bowl. He lunged to rescue the bowl that helped seal the treaty with Joshua, letting the broom flop down to hit the water jar next to the stand with a soft *thwack*.

Straightening and turning toward the deep voice and clipped words, he stuttered, "Y-yes, sir?" Keshub lowered his eyes when he recognized Phinehas, son of the high priest.

"I have need of your help."

"Me, sir?"

"Yes. I need you to guide me and some of the Levites to join Joshua. I am needed to apportion the spoils dedicated to the house of the Lord." The man frowned. His dark eyes never wavering.

"Report to me at the entrance of the Tabernacle before the sun rises. We will leave at the sun's rising. Do you understand?"

"Yes, sir. I will be at the Tabernacle before the sun comes up."

"Good. See that you are." Phinehas turned and strode back toward the imposing tent at the center of the Hebrew camp.

Keshub turned to the sun nearing the ridgeline. *Is Mr. Phinehas always so severe? God Most High, please help me.*

"[Joshua] *took up positions against* [Lachish] ... [and began observing the Sabbath at sundown.]" JOSHUA 10:31

Chapter 7
The Hill of Evil Counsel

At the Hebrew camp at Gilgal.   *Day 5*

In front of Joshua's tent, Keshub wrapped and tied his girdle at his waist. He topped his homemade sash with the leather belt and scabbard for his new-found Amorite sword. He sheathed the ... tool of death ... at his side.

The stench of battlefield cleanup haunted him. So many died in Aijalon Valley that day. *Thank you, God Most High, for Joshua's army that saved Gibeon from destruction. Bless Baba for his wisdom and courage to approach Joshua, not knowing if we would live or die. Thank you, God, for answering Joshua's prayer to stop the sun in its path. Thank you, Almighty God, that you listen to the prayers of men.*

Alerted at the sight of golden light creeping over the hills of Moab, Keshub rolled up the reed mat, stowed it in the tent, and tied the flaps closed. "I must not be late to meet Mr. Phinehas." He grabbed his slingstone bag and his knapsack bulging with his own and Master Joshua's stuff, downed water from his juglet, and jogged toward the Tabernacle entrance.

Mr. Phinehas emerged from the curtained sanctuary at the moment Keshub arrived. "It is good to see you are prompt, young man."

"Yes, sir."

"The Levites will join us." Ten men with long beards appeared, geared for travel, with their own knapsacks and walking sticks.

Keshub's stomach fluttered at the thought of travelling with such serious-looking gentlemen. *I must listen with care and speak when spoken to. No daydreams while trudging the path back to Gibeon—back home.*

* * *

Keshub searched for words, as he neared Jericho's spring. *Are they allowed to speak? Am I allowed to speak? What is expected of me?*

"Sir, it is always good to refill our water jugs whenever we have the opportunity. May I fill yours for you?"

The son of the high priest extended his water jug without a word. He had short nails and long fingers roughened by work. *What does a priest do all day?*

Keshub dipped the clay juglet into the swift-flowing water spewing from the earth and handed the dripping vessel back. "That is some of the best water you will ever taste, sir."

Mr. Phinehas turned his water flask to avoid drinking at a chip in its rim. After taking a long draught, he stifled a smile and wiped his lips with the back of his hand. He did not speak.

Keshub dropped his chin. He swallowed the question he dared not ask. *Mr. Phinehas and these men marched around the ruins of Jericho behind them. What a story they could tell.* "Sir, we go this way to the most beautiful valley in Canaan." Baba would know what to say. *And Baba will have a new water flask for you, too.*

CR&O

On the Hill of Evil Counsel across the bin-Hinnom from Jerusalem

Eskie stretched his legs, scaling the steep path. "Have you ever been over here before?"

Mando huffed behind him, "No, sir. No one I know comes here. I would have to cross the bin-Hinnom Valley to get here from Jerusalem."

"Who is this bin-Hinnom? Son of Hinnom? Why is the valley named for him?"

"Sir, I do not know. I only know the people of Jerusalem throw their garbage there and the king's men burn the garbage every few days to get rid of foul smells. No one else goes there, unless the king commands it. When he does, he commands all the common citizens to go, but the mothers in the king's palace hide their little ones and weep silently for days after."

Eskie nodded. "We are near the ridge. Stay low from here on up." He crouched beside an oak tree and crept forward, parallel to the crest line visible on his left through the trees. He gauged his steps to guess when the main city gate and Gihon Spring near it would be just over the peak.

Rounding a rocky shelf, he stopped and listened. No one here. Still he whispered. "What is this?"

Mando bumped into him from the back. "What?"

Eskie raised his hand for quiet. He did not want to miss anything. A deep double gash carved into a tree leered back at him, as he stood to full height. Lemon balm lay trampled around the base of the tree. A sharpened stake stained an ominous red slanted into the ground beside the tree. A single sandal lodged in a low-hanging, forked branch. Its long ankle cord dangled, stirred by the morning breeze. Lost? … Abandoned? … Not needed anymore?

He gulped.

Mando stood close by. Silent. Hardly breathing, he whispered, "It is true."

Eskie put an arm across the lad's shoulder. "What is true, Mando? You know what happened here?"

"We call this ... the Hill of Evil Counsel. They say terrible things happen here. Molech must live here."

"Why do you say that?"

"The double gash."

"You have seen it before?"

"Yes."

"Where?"

"In the king's palace ... in Molech's room we are never to go in."

"In a secret room?"

"The room is not secret. Everybody knows where it is, but we are never allowed to go in. There is a guard night and day." Mando waggled his head and smiled. "But I did."

Eskie chuckled. "You went in? Where was the guard?"

"He was flirting with a chambermaid in the room next door."

"What did you see?"

"Nothing."

"Was it dark?"

"No, there was a fireplace and a small fire."

"What did you mean when you said nothing was there?"

"Molech was not there."

"What else did you see in Molech's room in the king's palace?"

"Many bronze-tipped spears leaned against the near wall. Two criss-crossed stacks of clubs of war stood taller than me along another wall. On a pegged rack hung swords of all sizes. Their blades watched me. A wood column reaching to the ceiling stood in the middle of the room. A coil of rope and one chair by the fireplace. That is all, except for the double gashes painted in black tar on the rocks above the fireplace."

"Have you seen the double gash anywhere else?"

"There was a kind man who lived on the lane to the dung gate. He spoke to me every morning. Sometimes he paid me with fresh bread or dried fruit, when I carried out his slop jar. One day, the double gash appeared on his house beside his door … and no one ever saw him again."

"What do you think the double gash means?"

"It says, 'Molech was here.'"

Eskie tilted his head and shrugged one shoulder. He reached to dislodge the single sandal. "I wonder if a sandal maker could identify who this belongs to. I will keep it and show it to San-bar."

"Sir, do you think you should? What about Molech?"

"Mando, there is no Molech, no person, no god. My father says King Zedek uses the *idea* of Molech to carry out his evil plans and have power over his people. Our friend Jebus believes the same."

"Why would Jebus be in Zedek's army if he believes that?"

"Only because Zedek put Jebus's father in his dungeon to make bows and arrows for Zedek's army."

"Jebus's father is the bow maker?"

"Yes, you know him?"

"A very kind, soft-spoken man, and a hard worker."

"That sounds right. I saw him only once. Back to Molech, Zedek tried to get my father to make small pottery figures of Molech that he could sell so people would pray to them in their homes. But my father said no."

"Your baba said no to King Zedek?"

"Yes. Twice."

"Tw-ice?"

"Yes. He refused to make clay idols, and he refused to join Zedek's alliance. Instead, Baba took a delegation of Gibeonites to Gilgal. He asked Joshua for a treaty."

"Whoa! I wish I could have seen all that."

"My little brother did. He tended donkeys at the meeting at

Gilgal." Eskie dislodged the sandal from the tree. "In the end, my little brother became Joshua's slave in exchange for an alliance. My father paid a very large price, because he believes the God of the Hebrews is real. He knows Zedek's god is not."

"What do you think, sir?"

"I agree Molech is an idea made up by evil men. Whether the Hebrews' god is truth ... I am not sure what to think. What I know is, five days ago, the sun stood still over the Valley of Aijalon. Little brother was at Beth Horon Pass when Joshua asked his God to stop the sun. I keep wanting another explanation, but I have not found one. Baba and little brother believe in the Hebrew God. I do not know what to believe.

"I spent that very long afternoon with that vulture, Crabaw. We scavenged through the campsites of our army and the other four. We did not find much. It was a long afternoon, for sure."

Eskie pointed at a faint line in the dirt that led to the ridge of the Hill of Evil Counsel. "Whoever was murdered here ... recently, was dragged this way. Follow me, but stay down."

* * *

Lying flat, Eskie put his fist to his nose and cringed at the smell of death in the white smoke rising from bin-Hinnom wadi below. "What do you see across the way at Jerusalem?"

"The Gihon spring, people coming to get water, a few peddlers. Probably the usual ones, selling grape leaves, and mint, and vegetables. It is not market day."

"And the gate?"

"At the main double gate, there are always six guards. I see two outside, then two on the platform above the gate. Two more will be inside, but Zedek did not leave many of the best soldiers behind. Some are lame or sickly."

"What about the dung gate? Where is it?"

Mando pointed. "That way. Up the steep steps to the single door. Next to the two pine trees."

"How many guards there?"

"Only one. Only at night. Maybe not at all, with fewer men in Jerusalem."

"What about inside the walls? Where is the palace?"

"The largest stone house, surrounded by grape arbors on three sides."

"That is where you live?"

"Where I was born. Now I live in the barracks for soldiers."

"Where is that?"

* * *

Down below, the waters of Nephtoah beckoned. Eskie mulled over what he learned. Easy access through the dung gate in daytime, especially for Mando, perhaps Jebus's cousin, Xander, too.

Putting out his hand to grasp a rocky shelf beside the steep trail, he brushed a thorny, gray-green tzaleph bush, apparently growing from solid rock. Tender white and pink flowers bloomed on a thorny bush—its buds good for making pickles. He raised his hand to Mando.

"Let's collect the buds from all these pickle bushes. What will 'Zalef say when I give them to her?"

"[Joshua] *took up positions.* ...[All Israel began observing the Sabbath at sundown.]" JOSHUA 10:31

Chapter 8
The Sandal

Leading the high priest's
son to Aijalon Valley

Day 5,
continuing

Keshub shaded his eyes at the top of the long, steep climb from the Jordan Valley. The sun neared the Great Sea, with a gold and orange show just beginning. He swallowed down the lump in his throat at seeing his valley of Aijalon below. Had it been only five days earlier when he jolted awake on his family's rooftop? Golden-bearded Gadites sprang from predawn hiding places and led the Hebrews' charge against Gibeon's attackers.

"Sir, you can see the path to Gibeon clearly from here. May I run ahead and ask my father to meet you at the spring near our home?"

"Keshub ... is it?" Mr. Phinehas struggled to catch his breath.

"Yes, sir. Fifth son of the master potter of Ra-eef."

"The sun is near setting, and the Sabbath begins at sundown. Perhaps it would be better for us to make camp near that olive orchard below to observe the day of rest. Certainly, I would like to meet the noble man who came to Joshua with a desire to know the God who fights for Israel. Could you bring your father to speak with us?"

"Certainly. He will be delighted. May I bring you anything besides water from our spring?"

"Thank you, but no. We brought all we need. Fresh water would be appreciated, however."

* * *

Bearing a yoke of fresh water, Keshub angled his body into the climb. Water sloshed, with every step, back to the ledge, where he became a slave to Joshua. Ahead of him, Baba carried clean cloths and the simplest of foods to offer. Two moons ago, he and Baba had tensed for attack—waiting for the Hebrew army to arrive. Their lie about coming from a long distance to seek a treaty had come to light. Baba counted on Joshua to keep the treaty. *Perhaps Baba did not count on Joshua's demand for a slave to seal their treaty.*

Approaching the Levites, Baba bowed. His deep voice quickened Keshub's pride in his father. He believed him to be the wisest man in all their valley ... even in all of Canaan.

"Sirs, we welcome you to Aijalon Valley. We have fresh, cool water for you. Please allow us to serve you, as you take rest from your journey."

Phinehas acknowledged their hospitality with a slight bow. "Thank you, sir. We have your son to thank for guiding us here. He is a most mature young man for his age. You must be proud of him."

"I am, sir, as I am of all my sons." Baba turned to Keshub. "Fifth son, please set out the bread and hummus for our guests."

Keshub set the cloths on a large, flat rock and opened them to the Levites.

Baba took a position across from Mr. Phinehas. "Sir, I want

more than anything for you to teach me how to honor the God Most High on your Sabbath...."

⚭

Supper time at Nephtoah   *Day 5*

"Bur-r-r-umph." Eskie joined the hearty round of after-dinner belches and compliments to the cook, led by his host.

Za'atar, father of 'Zalef, belched a second time. "Eskie, thank you for providing two ducks for my homecoming meal. The fragrance hurried me along on the last leg of the journey. How did you manage to get a second duck? The flock usually takes flight after the first hit."

Eskie nodded in Jebus's direction. "Sir, I learned from your nephew, Jebus, a faster way of loading a second arrow. Also, I waited until a male duck was out of sight of the rest of the flock for my first hit. Then I had more than enough time to aim the second arrow."

Beside him, Mando frowned. "How did the duck not warn the others?"

Eskie tousled his new friend's head. "Because, Boy-dough, drakes do not have voices. He just wheezed once and floated, until I came back for him."

Jebus laughed with the rest, then cleared his throat. "Sir, I need to talk privately with you and Eskie, if I may. Surely, you know my father is in Zedek's prison. With the battle going badly for the Amorites and Zobar in charge in Jerusalem, I fear for Baba's life."

"Certainly. Let's move away from the heat of the fire circle to the knoll behind the house. There is usually a breeze from the sea by this time of evening.

Eskie nodded to Jebus. "Ask your man San-bar to join us."

* * *

Eskie found a log at the top of the rise, where a thick blanket of wood chips littered the area. He set his knapsack beside him and smiled at the chorus of frogs in the pond of Nephtoah.

Za'atar planted a torch beside Jebus and rolled up his own stool. "I take wood for bows to your baba in the palace dungeon every new moon."

Jebus clamped his mouth closed and blew out his cheeks, while pointing San-bar to share a log with him. "Yes, sir. Putting Baba in the dungeon was Zedek's way of *charming* me to stay in his army."

"From what I saw of Zedek in Gibeon, he is quite short on charm." Eskie swatted at a mosquito humming near his ear. "And it sounds like his son, Zobar, has even less."

Za'atar picked his teeth with the thin fibula of a duck's leg and tucked it in his girdle. "In truth, I was on the other end of the Valley of Rephaim, scouting for the perfect tree three days ago. An Amorite runner came by. I offered him a full flask of water and got some news. Zedek and the other four kings were executed that morning by the invaders at the cave of Makkedah. When the runner set out, the Hebrew army was attacking the city."

With the moon now rising from the Jordan Valley, Jebus bowed his head, elbows on his knees. "So now the son is king. His father and brothers were mean as snakes, but Zobar is a sadistic murderer. He may kill my father for revenge the moment he learns I survived the battle. Eskie, we have to free Baba as soon as possible."

Za'atar leaned forward. "We will do whatever it takes, nephew."

Eskie pulled the sandal from his knapsack. "I asked San-bar to join us to see if he knows who this belonged to."

Jebus examined the footwear. "It looks fairly new. Maybe San-bar made it." He thrust it in front of the cobbler, gesturing. "Have you ever seen this before?"

San-bar took the mass of crossing leather straps and held it to the light of the torch. He smiled and nodded and patted his chest several times with the flat of his palm. Giving the sandal back to

Jebus, the deaf sandal maker cupped both hands together at his waist, threw back his shoulders, and looked down his nose and scowled.

Eskie laughed, placing cupped hands at his own waist on top of the knot of his girdle. "That has to be Zedek. His big belt buckle with turquoise stones and his arrogant sneer—always staring others down."

San-bar shook his head no and waved two fingers.

"Number two? Zobar? His son?" Za'atar offered.

Vigorous shaking no and waving of two fingers still.

Jebus's tone grew somber. "Number two. Zedek's number-two man? The vizier? Zedek's advisor and second in command to Zobar, while his father led the army to conquer the Gibeonites. His vizier guarded the throne for Zedek's return. He did not foresee the Hebrews helping Gibeon."

San-bar pointed to the sandal and held up a single forefinger, with a question written on his face.

Jebus rasped, "Where did you get this, Eskie? Why is there only one?"

Eskie spat on the ground. "This sandal hung from the fork of an oak tree on the back side of the Hill of Evil Counsel. That is the name it is called among Zedek's household, according to our boy, Mando. A blood-stained spear stood beside the trunk scarred by a fresh double gash." Eskie bunched his fingers and drew two imaginary slash marks diagonally across his chest.

San-bar took in an audible gasp.

Jebus hit his chest with a fist and raised his eyes to the nearly full moon. Grief etched his face with shadow.

Eskie continued, "A single scraping line led from the tree of the double gash to the summit. There I detected a faint smell from bin-Hinnom below, like the battlefield cleanup stench in Aijalon Valley."

Eskie put his fist to his nose—remembering. "Whoever this

belonged to is surely dead now. Probably shown great disrespect by being beaten with his own sandal, tortured, then murdered by Molech's men of the double gash."

Jebus slumped. "Then we have *no* time. The vizier was the only sane person in the palace. Now they are all madmen. We must free my father—tomorrow—and we have no ally inside Jerusalem."

"How?" Eskie drew a rough circle in the sawdust. "We must have a plan to get inside the walls of Jerusalem, or it is a death wish."

"Jebus," Za'atar placed a calloused hand on his nephew's knee, "perhaps you do not know about your great uncle Jozman. A Jebusite in Jerusalem. Only a few among the elders do know. Joz has lived in Jerusalem, serving the Amorites since he was a boy. He is now in charge of taxing the vendors on market day and building and maintenance for the palace, the walls, and the streets. Most everything Zedek and his cohorts did not want to be bothered with."

Eskie leaned back. "Whoa! That is a foothold we can work with. Where does he live? Perhaps I can contact him."

Za'atar pointed at Eskie's circle on the ground. "Do you know where the dung gate is?"

Eskie jabbed at the circle with his stick. "Yes, Mando said it is here, near two pine trees. The main gate and the spring are here. Right?"

"Jozman's house is near the dung gate inside."

"Are you sure? Have you had contact lately?" Eskie leaned forward. "Mando told of a man who lived near the dung gate and who recently disappeared at the same time the sign of two gashes appeared on his home."

"Yes, I am sure. I saw Jozman at the last new moon. And I heard about the disappearance of Joz's friend and neighbor, the king's gardener, but that was several moons ago."

Eskie slapped both knees. "Perhaps I can talk to him tonight, if I leave now and can get in at the dung gate. Which house is his?"

Za'atar sketched in the sawdust. "Here. And lad, there is somewhere else I've seen the sign of the double gash." . . .

"[In position at Lachish …
the Sabbath day of rest.]" JOSHUA 10:31

Chapter 9
The Inside Man

After midnight in Jerusalem   *Day 6*

Eskie held his breath. Two pine trees and the dung gate, just ahead.

A soft who-hoot came from the top of the first pine tree. Eskie startled, as silent, white wings glided down into Jerusalem's cursed wadi bin-Hinnom.

Mando grasped Eskie's tunic and whispered, trembling. "Sir. The white owl is a very bad sign. We are doomed by Molech!"

Eskie half-turned to drape his arm on the young Amorite's shoulders. "Do not be afraid. You see, the old owl left, giving us permission to enter. He is not working for the Molech, who does not exist. Maybe he is watchman for us—to scare off the guard who was supposed to be at the gate."

Keeping to shadows, Eskie crept forward to the dung gate. *So did someone send the white owl to help us?*

Mando scampered up a set of rough stone steps.

Eskie followed, taking light steps, making no sound.

Mando reached for the leather handle.

Eskie froze in place, hoping the gate socket would be well greased with animal fat.

Mando gave a gentle push. The gate swung inward the length of a man's foot, before scraping on the hard-packed soil of the path on the other side. Mando eased through the narrow opening.

Eskie grabbed the hilt of his dagger and sucked in his belly, squeezing through the opening, with not a finger's width to spare. Inside, he leaned flat against the wall and listened. In the distance, he heard a loud guffaw in a deep male voice.

Mando whispered. "From the soldiers' quarters. Some of them gamble the goats' knuckles game all night."

Eskie pointed. "Let's go. You stay at the corner of the second lane and watch, until I signal to come. Understand?"

"Yes."

At a low-walled courtyard, Eskie pushed in a well-greased gate, making no sound. At the water crock, he used the flat side of his dagger to tap three times. He waited, then tapped twice.

A hen roosting inside the three-sided enclosure below the main house clucked her objection. Her sleepy rooster gave the midnight visitor a one-eyed stare.

"Hold on, old friend. We mean no harm." Eskie readied to tap the jar again.

"Who is there?" An older man's voice came from the roof's sleeping area.

Eskie cupped his hands at his mouth. "I have news from Za'atar at Nephtoah. We are friends. He told me to say 'arrow straight.'"

"Give me a moment."

Eskie waved at Mando to come over. A faint rustling above ended when a tamarisk-tree ladder lashed with goat's-hide strips descended from the second floor. "Come up."

Eskie shed his sandals and nodded to Mando to follow, as he climbed up. The lashings groaned, as they bore his weight. At the top, he entered the main house. An olive oil lamp the size of his palm burned in a far corner of the one-room dwelling. "Are you Jozman, Za'atar's kin?"

The man's eyes pierced his own, hesitating. Seeming satisfied, Jozman clasped strong hands on Eskie's forearms and leaned forward to place the traditional kiss to either cheek of the messenger from his nephew at Nephtoah.

"You are not Jebusite." He peered from beneath shaggy eyebrows.

Eskie extended a hand to Mando at the top rung of the ladder. "Sir. You know Mando. A grandson of Zedek. By the good fortune of a fall, he survived the Amorites' attack on Aijalon Valley. He is with me now. I am Gibeonite. The name is Eskie, third son of Ishtaba, master potter of Ra-eef.'"

"Sit here. We must keep our voices down." Jozman retrieved the oil lamp from the corner and set it in a Ra'eef' pottery dish in the middle of the mat. The low light in their midst cast faint shadows on the walls. Jozman placed a heavy cloak over the doorway to the narrow street.

Returning to sit, he began in a low voice, "We heard the battle did not go well for Zedek and the army. Why are you here?"

"I brought Jebus from Gibeon to Nephtoah's waters yesterday."

Jozman gasped. "Jebus survived?"

"Yes. And also Zander, a younger kinsman to you."

"My nephew's grandson. Thank you for this news. I have grieved over Zedek's execution by the Hebrews. Not for his sake, for I had nothing but contempt for the man. For the sake of my kinsmen who served him."

"Yes. Jebus sent us to make a plan to free his father from Zedek's dungeon … now Zobar's dungeon … as soon as possible."

"Jebus's father Mahnon is another nephew. How many men do you have with you?"

"Only a few. This young man and Zander, two able-bodied,

young men—younger than me, though, and San-bar, the deaf shoemaker. Plus, Jebus, who received a vicious blow to his head. It is a wonder he survived the battle and now the trek to stay with Za'atar. I fear he needs many days to return to full strength—and to see better. He is seeing double."

"Zobar's band of left-behind soldiers is not much better. Now that Zedek's vizier is missing, there is no sane, reasoning person in the palace to advise the new ruler."

"Sir, I have information about the vizier. He is surely at the bottom of bin-Hinnom. Mando and I found his sandal hanging in a tree earlier today on the other side of the Hill of Evil Counsel. The sandal maker identified it. And the tree bore fresh marks of the double gash."

Jozman dropped his chin to his chest a moment, before going on, "I was afraid of that. I saw Jebus's father two days ago when I delivered a supply of pine resin for glue. He is sick with worry for his son, but he continues to work, making fine bows. Otherwise, Zobar would have no use for him and would give him no light or food."

Eskie jerked his head toward the street below and cautioned with a sudden movement of his hands for quiet.

Jozman and Mando froze in place.

"Old man! Wake up!"

The chickens squawked a protest.

Jozman smothered the oil lamp, stood, and filled the open doorway. Starlight shone beyond him.

In total darkness, Eskie clamped a hand on Mando's knee, willing him to make no sound.

"Who is there?" Jozman's deep, calm voice betrayed no fear.

"We come with news from Zobar the king, old man. A runner has come. Lachish is shut up tight and is surrounded by the Hebrews. They expect attack tomorrow at dawn."

"Aye, old man, *the king* orders you to build a tower of Molech at dawn." The second man slurred his words together.

"At dawn? With no preparations made at this point, it will take at least three days. Tell him that."

"Tell him yourself, old man. He is not in a mood to hear no from anyone."

"Then tell him I will begin preparations at dawn and will speak with him at noon. Also tell him I need six men in the morning to begin the work."

"We will tell him the good news. You will start at dawn. He will have to hear the bad news from you."

Jozman waited until the sound of their shuffling feet and their arguing about which one of them would deliver the good news faded into the night.

Eskie counted on his fingers. "Sir, it is unlikely the Hebrews will attack Lachish this morning."

"What makes you say that?"

"They take a day of rest every seven days. Tomorrow is the day they call the Sabbath. I think they will not attack tomorrow."

"Strange."

"Yes, sir. It is."

"Perhaps that gives us another day before Zobar demands the impossible. You young men have come at just the right time. I have a job for you." Jozman uncovered the window to let in faint moonlight.

Eskie touched Mando's knee. "Mando, go down to Mr. Jozman's courtyard and be watchman for us. Keep in shadow."

"Lachish ... [the Sabbath day of rest.]" JOSHUA 10:31

Chapter 10
The White Owl

Near first light at Jerusalem   *Day 6*

Eskie flattened himself into shadow against a stacked-stone house. He spread a hand on Mando's chest, signaling for quiet. Peering around the corner, he snapped back.

A night guard stood next to the dung gate. *Now what? We are finished in Jerusalem. If only we can get out the way we came in without being seen.*

Who-hoot.

Eskie tensed. Hand on Mando's trembling chest.

"The ghost owl, sir?"

Who-hoot.

Eskie chanced another look around the corner toward Zobar's man and the gate. Brave guardian of Jerusalem hiked his tunic in one hand. He secured his turban with the other and scampered along the outer wall toward the soldiers' barracks.

"Heh, heh, Mando. It is just as I said before. The owl is *not* a bad-luck sign. He is there to help us. Let's go."

Creeping out of the dung gate with the smallest opening

possible, Eskie paused.

Who-hoot.

"Mando, we have a friend who is watching over us." … *I thought I was being funny, but maybe we do. If true, does the One who named the stars also direct the owl?*

"Ready, Boy-dough?" Eskie raised the hood of Jozman's worn-out cloak and bent at the waist. He jabbed the oaken handle of his borrowed hoe onto the rocky ground. Palming the flat stone head, he leaned on it and hobbled down the steps to the road leading to the main gate. He cast his eyes downward and grimaced, as if in extreme pain. He concentrated on imitating Uncle Yaakoub's gait with his injured knee.

"Hey, Cripple! Where are you going so early?"

"To our Kidron garden, sir." Mando spoke for them, while Eskie leaned harder on his upended garden tool.

Around the bend in the road, Eskie straightened. "Let's go quickly now. You lead the way. First light will be upon us soon." He slid down the rocky incline to the trickling, dry-season wadi.

Mando led up another wadi, with not enough water to wet their sandals. A cock crowed, welcoming a faint light from Moab creeping over the horizon.

Eskie knew the sounds and smells of early-morning industry. Coals banked overnight glowed with new tinder and kindling added. Water pots heated among the coals. Sandaled feet scritch-scratched here and there in courtyards, while a rooster with a droopy cockscomb gave him an unblinking eye.

Mando quickened his step. "Mr. Naqib, the arrow smith, lives just around this bend."

"Point out which gate and wait yonder, until I give you a wave." Eskie removed a sling stone from the bag at his side and palmed its smoothness. When Mando pointed out the gate, Eskie rapped three times with the stone.

The sound of sandals approached the other side, and a fist-sized portal at eye level opened. A dark eye topped with the bushiest eyebrow Eskie had ever seen squinted at him.

"Good morning, sir. I come with a message from a certain man of Jerusalem and your own nephew Jebus. *'Arrow straight'.*"

A cock crowed, as the bar inside slid to unlock. Bronze hinges creaked.

"Who are you?"

"I am Eskie, third son of Ishtaba of the Ra'eef' potters of Gibeon. Perhaps you have heard news that Zedek and four kings of the Amorites were defeated in Aijalon Valley five days ago."

"Yes. I heard. What about my nephew Jebus?"

"He is alive. Injured, but alive. He is with your kin at the waters of Nephtoah now. Za'atar sends greetings."

"I see. Come in." Naqib pointed with an open hand to the fire and the steaming water pot. "And your friend?"

"This is Mando. One of Zedek's unlikely soldiers who, by some good providence, survived the battle, too." *There I go again.* "Your kinsman, Xander, is also at Nephtoah. He was ill with the runs and missed the battle—Zedek's bad meat."

Naqib dropped his chin to his chest. "Good providence, indeed. Xander is my grandson. What do you know about the sun standing still that day?"

"I know I saw my shadow stop at my feet for the longest time, as you did, too. Right?"

Naqib nodded, extending a clay bowl of rosemary tea.

"My little brother has served the leader of the Hebrews since my father tricked them into making a treaty with us. Perhaps you heard that, too."

"I did. The Gibeonites' alliance with the invaders caused great alarm among the Amorites. Zedek stockpiled weapons for many moons. Then he arrested my brother, Mahnon, to gain control of the archers' process, and Jebus had no choice but to join Zedek's army. But go on, please."

"Yes, sir. My little brother, just ten harvests plus three, was with Joshua at the pass of Beth Horon, when his men were chasing the Amorites. My brother heard Joshua pray. He asked the god of the Hebrews to stop the sun from going down until they caught all the fleeing enemy."

Eyebrows lowered, Naquib squinted and stared. "How can anyone fight that kind of army?"

"A good question, sir, but, for now, Mr. Jozman has a plan. He will deal with the new tyrant of Jerusalem and free your brother from Zobar's dungeon. Mr. Jozman sends this message...."

* * *

"Come, I will show you a shortcut over Mt. Moriah to the valley of the cheesemakers on the other side. You will not have to go by Jerusalem to get to Nephtoah from there. Someone here will return Jozman's things to him."

"Thank you." Eskie nudged Mando. "Hey, Boy-dough. Wake up. Time to go."

Naqib led out in full sunshine up the trickling wadi. He pointed to a steep trail angling to the top of Mt. Moriah, above the walled city of Jerusalem.

"If you see my great-uncle 'Raunah at his threshing floor, give him this bag of apricots. Here is one for 'Zalef. We will meet again in two days—to celebrate the opening of the Jerusalem marketplace under King Zobar."

"Yes, sir. I will be there."

* * *

Eskie dragged his open hand down his face and yawned. Already, the sun at their backs showed midmorning. The visits with Jebus's uncles yielded a solid plan. Eskie turned the plan over and over in his mind. He came to Jerusalem to free Jebus's father from Zobar's dungeon. He did not foresee helping in a Jebusites' takeover of Jerusalem, too. What would Baba say?

He and Mando descended the sunset side of Mt. Moriah. He stopped with the cheesemakers' valley below. "Mando, let's sit a while and eat one of Mr. Naqib's apricots. Here is one for you."

He rubbed his apricot with the tail of his girdle and took a bite. "Mando, do you know the liveryman who lives down there beside the caravanners' trail from Gibeon?"

"Not really. Except for carrying slop to the Hinnom. I did not often go outside Jerusalem's walls."

"Then we have one more stop to make before heading back to Nephtoah. I need to talk to the liveryman who lives yonder. He is an old friend of my uncle."

* * *

Eskie upended his water flask at the Nephtoah Spring and refilled it. "Mando, I could sleep all day. I will clean up a little here before going on to Za'atar's place. Go on ahead if you want. I will be there in a bit.

… Refreshed, Eskie regirded while considering the short conversation with the liveryman. Something about Uncle Yaakoub's friend puzzled him, but he could not decide why. He sauntered toward the house with wet hair.

On a stump in the courtyard, Pickle Girl made fast work of shelling a basket of fava beans beside her.

Eskie slowed and trod with light steps, until he neared the low wall surrounding the house. He placed two fingers in his mouth … *Squee-ee-yew!*

Pickle Girl jumped and upended the smaller basket of shelled beans in her lap. She glared at him over her shoulder, her eyes flashing. "See what you made me do?"

Eskie bowed slightly. "I am certainly sorry I surprised you and made you jump, though it was kind of funny."

She rose and her fists went to her hips. Her head jerked aside. "It was not funny at all, and now I have to pick these favas up and wash them."

"May I help?"

"No. You would just be in the way." 'Zalef stooped and turned over her basket to refill it.

"Will this help?" Eskie extended a rough-woven, flaxen bag bulging with its contents.

"What is it?" Frowning, she peeked into the bag and suddenly smiled with delight. "Apricots!"

"From your kin Naqib in the valley of craftsmen. He also sent a bar of the olive oil soap his wife makes. He gave me a small nub of it and suggested I try it—though I cannot imagine why. Say, may I sleep on your rooftop today? I have hardly slept in the past several nights."

Pickle Girl turned away, before replying, "Your gear is on the third step." Turning back, her tone softened. "Have you eaten?"

"Uh, I had an apricot."

"Well, stay right there while I get you something."

In a moment, she reappeared from the house with a small Ra-eef' bowl covered with a linen cloth. "Eat this. It is all I have prepared for now." She ducked her head and retreated.

Eskie folded back the cloth. "Ah, capers and pickled duck eggs!" *Pickle Girl, I could get used to this.*

"Joshua … attacked [Lachish]." JOSHUA 10:31

Chapter 11
A Rare Smile

At Beth Horon Pass   *Day 7*

From the height of the pass at Beth Horon, Keshub paused and gulped from his water flask. He pointed to the rock Joshua stood on. "Sir, this is where Joshua prayed seven days ago for God Most High to stop the sun from going down. The Amorite armies were escaping. Did you notice how long that day was?"

A rare smile lit up Mr. Phinehas's face. He nodded and turned about, raising both arms. "God Most High, I praise your holy name! You dwell with your people between the cherubim in the Holy of Holies, but your spirit and your power cannot be contained. Bless your servant Joshua this day."

His arms dropped to his side, and he bowed his head. A moment later, he turned back to Keshub and spoke in a hushed tone, nodding. "I did notice. So that is what happened. Thank you, Keshub, for telling me."

"Yes, sir. Some of Joshua's men found the five kings of the Amorites hiding in a cave at Makkedah." Keshub pointed below the pass. "Joshua told them to seal up the cave and to keep pursuing the rest so they would not escape to their walled cities. That is when Joshua told me to go back to Gilgal. I do not know what happened here after that. I know the sun did not go down for about another day."

"You did not arrive at Gilgal that day. Why?"

"Sir, when I returned to Gibeon, my gran-mamaa was dying. I spent the rest of that afternoon telling her the stories I learned from Joshua about God Most High. She took her last breath, as the sun came up the next morning, comforted by the God who knows us and who listens to the voices of men." Keshub swallowed a lump and bit his lip.

He turned back to point at the Gibeon hill. "We placed her beside Gran-baba that day above the threshing floor. Gran-baba always hoped to learn about the One who named the stars."

Phinehas nodded and raised an arm to the sky. "Our God is the Almighty, all-knowing God and Creator." He bowed his head and placed his hand over his heart. "The most awesome thing about our God is that he knows our hearts and hears our every word. Every one."

"Yes, sir."

* * *

Keshub handled a rough-barked branch of an oak and stomped on its midsection to break it in half. Tossing the pieces onto a pile nearby, he spied a runner coming his way from Lower Beth Horon. The runner drew near, and Keshub grasped his water flask, ready to offer it. "Hallow! Do you need some water?"

The runner stopped, panting. "Yes, thank you."

Eskie extended his juglet. "Where are you headed?"

"Gezer. King Horam. *Gulp.* A message from Lachish."

"A walled city, I hear. One of the best, right?"

"Yeah, used to be. But, right now, the city is surrounded by

Hebrews. Hey, thanks for the water, lad. I must go now." He nodded and thrust the flask back, then waved, and off he went.

Keshub gazed after him. *Thank you, sir, for the information. Now we know where Joshua is. God Most High, please protect Joshua and give him success.*

☾☙☽

At the pond of Nephtoah

Eskie whisked a flying pest at his ear and lay in wait for his prey—silent. He glanced left, where Dubo and Dagan peered through the same screen of green.

Within reach on the other side, Mando's grin stretched wide. He pointed. He had prey in sight.

Thumbs up from Dubo and Dagan.

Eskie raised to his elbows without a sound, shifting to one. He counted with raised fingers—eyes on his target—one … two … three. Lunge! Both hands shot out, lancing through the reeds. Clamping on the biggest and fattest croaker of them all. Cold and wet to the touch, the strong legs attempted to leap away, paddling at nothing but air. *No, sir. You are invited to dinner, and I will not take no for an answer.*

Thrashing in the low growth to his left, someone wrestled with his quarry. Warned not to scare others off, Dubo and Dagan followed orders better than Mando. He hissed through clenched teeth, attempting quiet. "Sir! I got one! Whoa, fellow, you are mine. … No, no, stop."

Splash!

"Aw-w. Sir, he got away."

Eskie chuckled low. "All right, Boy-dough. You will get another chance. Dagan, let's take care of these two and see if we can get enough for supper." He squeezed his hands together, with his fat little friend kicking with all his might. Leaning on both elbows, he brought his lower extremities to a crawling position. With a grunt, he raised himself to kneeling and got up with a crooked smile. "Frog hunting is probably not something kings and noblemen do. It is much too undignified." He shook himself to settle his tunic into its proper place without use of his hands. "They do not know what fun they are missing. Right, Boy-dough?"

Eskie rendered his leggy catch immobile. He dropped him in the reed basket he had coaxed 'Zalef to loan him. Maybe she would not mind too much when she found out he filled it with frogs.

...

"I got it! I got it!" Mando could not contain his excitement for his first catch.

"Sh-h-h!"

...   .

Eskie and Dubo carried the full basket between them, matching their steps. "Mando, go on ahead and find Miss 'Zalef. Tell her we got her a basketful of frogs for supper."

Mando darted ahead, calling out, "Miss 'Zalef, Miss 'Zalef!"

Dagan gave him a nudge on the shoulder. "You coward. You did not tell Miss 'Zalef we were going frog hunting, did you?"

"No, she will be surprised, but maybe she will be sweet to Mando. You know, with him being an orphan and all."

Dubo laughed. "I hope you can talk her into cooking them for us."

"Oh, I thought we could cook them. They are much too much trouble to ask her to cook."

"Us?" Dagan scowled. "Have you done this before?"

"Sure. When my brothers and I were about Mando's age, we did this."

Dubo dipped his chin and frowned at Eskie. "What do they taste like?"

Eskie shrugged. "Kind of like chicken. But the most fun is cooking them. They dance."

"What?" Dubo and Dagan chimed in together.

"You will see."

* * *

Eskie swallowed hard and smiled his broadest. He had seen Miss 'Zalef's wide stance before.

With fists on her hips, she lowered her chin and glared. "Eskie. You did not say you would put *frogs* in my basket."

Eskie turned his head aside and addressed her with a hopeful smile. "I thought you might say no, but I am hoping you will like frog's legs with your supper." Hurrying on, he nodded. "We will cook them, too. You will see. It will be fun, and you will like them."

"Fun, hunh?" She softened—ever so little—fists still at her hips. "You will not make a mess in my kitchen."

"No, ma'am." Eskie smiled … and wheedled. "We will build a fire outside your courtyard and let it burn down to coals. We will string the frogs' legs on soaked willow stems and suspend them over the coals. All we need from you is a little olive oil and that wonderful spice mixture your baba loves."

She looked at his muddy feet and raised her eyes to his. "And when will you bathe?"

Eskie looked down his front. "Aw-w, man. I took a bath yesterday."

"Well, you all smell like frogs today."

"Yes, ma'am. We will take care of that. Thank you." Eskie winked.

Her eyes flared, and she turned, scurrying to the house.

Eskie stifled a laugh. "Let's get to work, men."

His men shoved him and had the good sense to chuckle softly.

* * *

Sitting cross-legged across the coals from Mando, Eskie grasped a soaked willow strand in each hand. Mando took the other ends.

Dubo and Dagan had two more stringers of frogs' legs suspended between them. "Hold tight. Do not let them fall into the ashes. Keep them moving a little so the willow does not dry out and burn."

"When will they dance?" Mando's eyes were wide, expectant.

Dubo and Dagan eyed each other, smirking and shaking their heads.

"Mando, we can lower our lines a little so they get more heat. They will begin to dance when they get hot enough." At the corner of his eye, 'Zalef took her position at her standing loom in the courtyard. He glanced her way, and she ducked her head to fidget with something in her lap.

Dubo smirked. "Eskie, tell us about the confusion you stirred up on your little brother's first day at the spies' perch."

Eskie chuckled. "Oh, I just stretched the truth a little when I introduced my ten-plus-two- year-old brother."

Dubo nodded. "Yes, you did. The way you told it, he was a great hunter and captured a band of robbers all by himself. Finally, we asked his brother about all this. Keshub said he did kill a lion attacking his sheep one day, but he just scared off a bear."

Eskie tried to look innocent.

Dagan bit his lip.

"And the band of robbers was just one." Eskie shrugged, and his voice trailed off. He had not intended to bring up the subject of Dagan's father, with Dagan sitting there.

"Look! I see one dancing. See that? There he goes again!" Mando's delight rescued the moment. Eskie glanced at 'Zalef. She watched with open curiosity.

Dubo laughed. "Eskie, I thought sure this would be one of your great tricks. But twitching like that on a string does make a strange, little line dance."

Eskie grinned at 'Zalef across the way, staring in surprise. He caught her eye and winked again.

She smiled and bent her head low.

"The Lord handed Lachish over to Israel,..." Joshua 10:32

Chapter 12
Jerusalem Market and the Rescue

Nephtoah   *Day 8*

Eskie rolled over on Za'atar's rooftop, rousing from a dream of frogs' legs and pickled duck eggs. His eyes flew open.

Today is the day I need providence on my side. Star Namer, sir, I do not know how this works. But if you are God Most High, you cannot be happy with Zedek's Molech contraption and his feeding the fire with small children.

I still do not know if I believe in you or how to believe in you. Perhaps you will show me. For today, I need all the help I can get to do my part to rid Jerusalem of the rats who infest that noble city.

"Eskie!"

"Coming!" Eskie bounded up and rolled and tied his blankets in place and sat on them, while tying on his worn sandals. He skittered down the steps from the roof and splashed water on his face and hands.

Jebus and the others already sat at Za'atar's reed mat. As Eskie sank into the place saved for him at Za'atar's right, his daughter brought a basket of fresh, warm flat bread. Eskie's right hand came unbidden to cover his heart.

'Zalef lowered her eyes and stood close by. Sucking in her dimples, she waited for the basket to round the circle of eight men and return empty. *She must have started cooking during third watch!*

Eskie followed the lead of Za'atar and took a grape-leaf bundle from the serving bowl. *Umm-mm.* He closed his eyes to chew the savory bundle and brought his empty hand to his chest again before taking another.

* * *

Geared up, Eskie went over the day's plan. They would arrive at bin-Hinnom by noon. Dagan, Dubo, Xander, and San-bar would go to Jozman's tower to help finish the work and stand guard, until time for action.

"Jebus, if you begin to feel weak, we have Jozman's place for you to rest."

"Man, I would not miss any of this, no matter what."

"Then let's go, men. May providence be on our side."

"Hear, hear!"

Eskie and Jebus brought up the rear.

"Eskie."

"Yes?" He turned to the soft-spoken voice.

"Take this vittles bag with you and be safe." 'Zalef thrust a small bag into his hand.

Her brief touch raced through him, as he tucked her gift into his girdle. Turning back to Jebus, his friend smiled.

With eyebrows raised, Jebus led out. "To Jerusalem, Eskie."

Eskie cleared his throat. "Yes, *the plan.*"

* * *

With Jerusalem around the next bend in the road, Eskie scanned the trails funneling travelers toward Jerusalem.

Mando pointed. "Look, sir. I see a camel coming. Is that a caravanner?"

"Good eyes, Mando. Coming from the direction of Gibeon, too."

Up ahead, Dubo gave a casual salute, before leading his men into the bin-Hinnom Valley.

Going on, Eskie halted near the two pine trees and turned toward oncoming travelers to distract them. He spoke under his breath, "Go now, Jebus."

To fellow travelers, "Good day to you. Where are you folks from?" ... ...

"Eskie?"

Eskie twisted his neck toward a familiar voice. "Ya-yah'!"

His brother by marriage walked beside his camel, loaded to almost twice its height with goods. Moving to the side of the road, the former caravanner embraced him cheek to cheek and stepped back. "Your baba was hoping we would see you—and here you are the first person we meet in Jerusalem."

"Did you bring pottery to market?"

"We did. And your farmer cousin sends cheese and leather goods. Agh-taan sends olive oil. We also have newly harvested wheat and flax cloth."

Eskie looked back up the trail. "Is that Lehab leading two donkeys? Lehab!"

"Eskie!"

"Can I help you set up? This is my new friend, Mando. We can both help."

* * *

"Ah, Ra-eef' pottery from Gibeon!" A neighbor vendor came

by. "Were you there for that battle that happened recently? How is my friend Yaakoub?"

"Yes, sir, I was there. My uncle Yaakoub injured his knee and may never hike to Jerusalem again, but he is still telling his stories—and collecting new ones."

* * *

Eskie scratched the back of his head. If he told the story once, he told of the day the sun stood still more times than the number of his fingers and toes. For those who asked, Eskie gave news of the Hebrews. "The latest word is they were expected to attack Lachish yesterday. No news since."

Itching for *the plan* to go into action, Eskie strolled through the market area. He found Naqib's mat stacked with flint knives, scrapers, olive oil soap, and garden produce. Eskie picked up a small arrow with a flint tip just right for frog hunting. With two hands, he held one at eye level and nodded a greeting.

Naqib leaned forward. "'*Arrow straight*'. Everything is in place here."

Eskie laughed aloud. "Yes, sir. It is a very fine day."

Jozman appeared from the main gate with two of Zobar's soldiers. At the sunrise side of the market area, they attached woven-reed target mats to a rope suspended between two trees.

Shrill whistles from the bridge above the main gate quieted the crowd a moment. The new king appeared head and shoulders above the wall.

Jozman addressed the crowd. "Gentlemen, the king has arranged a special day for your entertainment. For all who have a vendor's space, we will come to collect your fee soon. Each payment will give you entrance into either the slingshot or archery contests. Winners will receive a myrtle-wreath crown, a reduced fee today, and no fee at our next market day in seven days. The competition line begins here. Do not forget King Zobar is providing free stuffed grape leaves for everyone after the games."

The crowd shouted and cheered. The new king waved and smiled, like a beloved, benevolent monarch, which he was not. Eskie smirked and located Mando. He gave him a quick nod and eased to the back of the crowd, to Ya-yah's and Lehab's booth.

"Eskie, will you enter the archery contest for our booth?"

"Cousin, you are quite good yourself now. You do not need me." Smiling ear to ear, Eskie winked at the young cousin he mentored as they hunted the duck ponds of Aijalon Valley. Through his teeth, he voiced, "I cannot. I have a job to do."

* * *

Inside the city wall, Eskie passed two houses, with young children playing and the sound of pottery warp weights clattering in the breeze. Three women with sad, hollow faces wove flax cloth on standing looms in the adjoining courtyard. *Did their husbands die at Gibeon?*

At Jozman's house, cheers from the games outside the city surged. Eskie knocked on the water jar in the courtyard—reminded of the urgency of *the plan.* "Jebus. Time to go."

Jebus emerged from semidarkness in the second floor living quarters. "Let's hurry."

Eskie could not disagree. "Mando, lead us to the dungeon by the way least likely to encounter opposition."

"Yes, sir. Follow me." Mando led them to a narrow street darkened from the midday sun by its second floors and overhanging balconies. A merchant street.

Eskie flexed his right hand, ready to draw his bronze dagger, but the narrow passage presented only closed doors on either side. At the end of the street, bright sunlight beckoned through a stone archway onto a broader street.

Mando whispered, "The palace is across that street."

Eskie tugged on Mando's girdle and took the lead. He stopped in a shadowed niche behind the arch. The wall on this side of the palace had one gate midway.

Mando tugged Eskie's girdle. "Inside that gate is a grape arbor, a path to the kitchen door, and the dungeon."

Beside the gate stood one soldier with a spear, baking in the full sun of afternoon.

Inside the passageway in deep shadow, Eskie drew a smooth fist-sized stone from his bag. He tensed, waiting for just the right timing, barely breathing. ... The Amorite turned and leaned a shoulder to the wall beside the door ... and stuck his hand in the bag over his shoulder.

Eskie wound up and hand-launched his stone with a *whirr* and a *thwack*.

The guard reeled backward, encountered the wall with out-stretched arms, and crumpled to the ground. The stone clattered and rolled on the stone-paved street.

"You finished him with one stone, sir!"

"Sh-h-h."

Jebus nodded. "Good throw. Let's go."

Mando scampered to pick up the stone and tucked it into his own bag.

Inside the palace garden, no other guard stood in their way. He unsheathed his dagger and led the way. Taking a peek through the door, a hallway extended to his left. The chatter of the kitchen maids wafted through an arched opening halfway down. The comforting fragrances of leeks, garlic, and familiar spices tickled his nose.

Mando slid between him and and the door and pointed to a dark doorway at the end of the hall. "The root cellar ... and the dungeon."

Eskie nodded. "Jebus, we will walk past the kitchen door as if we belong here. Maybe the cooks are so busy they will not notice us. You take the inside."

Through the kitchen doorway, a whole flock of women worked feverishly, folding grape leaves over savory bits. Eskie's mouth watered.

At the opening to the cavern below, the dank air told of fermenting wine, stored root vegetables, and human waste.

Mando straightened his shoulders and whispered, "Who takes out the slop since I have been gone?"

Eskie smiled and adjusted his knapsack. "Wait here. If any danger comes your way, throw my stone down the stairs of the dungeon to warn us—and run."

"Ready, Jebus?"

"Yes."

Eskie entered the foul-smelling, gaping darkness. He pierced the fetid air with his weapon, swiping cobwebs aside. The spear warned him of the next step. The air cooled, becoming no less oppressive. The tunnel turned right, and a clay oil lamp in a recess of the wall made a dim point of light in overwhelming darkness. Dampness clung to the wall.

At a landing, Eskie's dagger hand found no wall.

"Joshua took [Lachish]... *on the second day."* JOSHUA 10:32

Chapter 13
The King and His Henchmen

The Battle for Jerusalem   *Day 8*

Momentarily off balance, Eskie's senses told him wine fermented in the darkness there.

Jebus whispered, "Root cellar over here."

Turning left, Eskie wished he had another hand to pinch his nose. Returning to fresh air and sunshine could not come soon enough. Dim light came from another turn in the deepening passageway, Jebus broke ahead and rushed to his father's side.

Eskie crouched, ready.

A torch dipped in tar attempted to light the oppressive darkness. Searching out the shadowed recesses, Eskie found no one. He turned back to Jebus and his father.

Mahnon lay on the cold, clammy floor of his cell, with his knees clasped to his chest. His body shook with chills. His teeth chattered.

Eskie spied the prisoner's water jar—empty. His slop jar stood full. Rodent droppings surrounded a dirty food bowl.

"Eskie. Help me get Baba out of here." Jebus' voice broke, as he bent over his father.

Mahnon's shackles attached to a bronze chain anchored him to the wall. Eskie sheathed his dagger and hammered at the base of a bronze stake with the blunt end of the spear. Wedged deep in a crack in solid limestone, little by little, the stake broke loose.

Eskie yanked the torch from its holder. The smoke burned his eyes, making the stench more bearable. "Here, you take the spear and torch. Lead us up. I will carry your baba."

Jebus agreed with a nod and grabbed the smoky light.

Eskie knelt and clasped the sick man to his breast. Mahnon weighed considerably less than his son had a few days ago, even with the added weight of bronze shackles and a chain.

At the top of the stairs, Jebus seated the butt of the flickering flame in another wall sconce and grabbed the chain chattering after Eskie.

Eskie carried the bowman straight to the exit into the heat of day. At a bench and the grape arbor, dappled shade provided relief. He lowered Jebus's father and gave him water from his flask.

Jebus laid the spear and chain aside and charged back into the palace.

"Where is he going?" Mando stared after him.

Jebus disappeared behind the heavy door into the kitchen hallway.

"Mando, is that a pool yonder? Take my head wrap and wet it and bring it back. The chills are less, but I fear a fever will follow."

"Yes, sir."

Eskie held his flask to the bowmaker's lips and helped him drink. Mando returned, and he mopped the sick man's brow. *I wish I knew more to do for him.*

Jebus returned with a wine juglet and a pottery bowl, and leading a young woman wearing a kitchen smock. She carried a water jar and flat bread.

"Jebus, we must take your baba to a better place. Follow me."

Eskie stooped to pick up Mahnon. "Mando, stay here and watch for us."

"Yes, sir."

* * *

Eskie rejoined Mando. "Jebus is staying with his father. We almost arrived too late. Now capturing the king is up to us, Boy-dough. I was counting on Jebus, but he is needed here. Besides that, I think he was feeling weak again. Perhaps a headache, too. I wonder. What can I do now? We need more help. ... Mando?"

"Yes, sir?"

"Can you get down the wall into the Hinnom and back up again?"

"Yes, sir."

"Tell Dagan and Dubo to come with you and bring ...."

* * *

After sharing his pickled duck egg with Jebus and his father, Eskie returned to the dung gate. Mando, Dubo, and Dagan slipped through. He drew in a deep breath and blew it out with puffed cheeks. He clasped each of his Gibeonite friends to him in a dou-ble-cheek welcome. "Men, Jebus had to stay with his father. It is up to us now to make this happen. You brought the rope?"

Dubo raised a rough reed guffa basket.

"Good. Are we ready?"

"We are."

Eskie turned and crept along the outer wall toward the main gate ... Their steps crunched the gravel. "Dubo, Dagan." With the king's position in sight, Eskie sidestepped deeper into the shadow, while the two came close.

"Go down this lane away from the wall, circle over, and come back to the wall on the other side of the main gate. Mando and I will wait, until you are in position. Then we will get the attention of the two guards. You two will rush Zobar and restrain him. Understand?"

They nodded.

"I will see you yonder in a bit. Wait for us to engage the two guards first, before climbing the stairs to Zobar. Let's see if we can surprise the king out of his sandals."

. . .   . . .

Eskie fidgeted in the shade of an oak growing next to the outer wall. Turning a sling stone over and over in his hand, he waited. At the spring outside the city, Jozman finished the sling-stone competition and neared the end of the archery match—wrestling next.

Mando nudged him. "There they are, sir. Dagan and Dubo are in place."

"Thanks, man. We will bide our time a little longer." Eskie put up an open hand to signal *stay. Wait.* He handed the spear to his young friend and explained how to use it.

The crowd cheered with great enthusiasm on the other side of the wall.

In his mind, Eskie checked off every step of *the plan*, as he listened for his cue to action.

Jozman got the crowd's attention, and they quieted. "Gentle countrymen, we will end today's games with wrestling. Any man willing to try will be eligible to gain a sword, a shield, and a bag of wheat, by edict of King Zobar." *So Zobar liked Jozman's idea to end with wrestling. Good.*

"O-h-h-h!"

"Hurrah!"

Shrill whistles sounded from Zobar's hefty guards flanking him above the main gate. The crowd quieted.

King Zobar bellowed to the crowd below. "Hear ye! Faithful

soldiers of the king's guard will also compete. May the best man win!" *Just as planned, Zobar, old man. We knew you could not resist trying to keep it all for yourself.*

"Aw-w-w." The crowd, as one, moaned. No cheers. *Uh-hunh. Nobody loves a bully.*

Eskie pictured it happening. Five of the king's royal guard strutted to circles Jozman had marked in the dirt. Timid boos confirmed his opinion. Zobar's soldiers had few friends in the community. He wished he could have fought them. But he had a more important mission. *"What would Pickle Girl do if I came back all black-eyed and bruised?"*

Jozman repeated the invitation. "Gentlemen, we now have five protectors of Jerusalem ready to compete. Who else will step forward to fight for a sword, a shield, and a bag of wheat?"

. . .

"Oh-h-h!"

"Yeah!" The crowd approved.

"Wha-a?"

Eskie chuckled under his breath.

"Gentlemen, we now have five more contenders. These young men are humble craftsmen … three stoneworkers … and … two blacksmiths. We are ready to begin!"

Eskie smiled through clamped teeth … ready to launch the takeover … as another part of the plan came together.

The market-day crowd voiced their approval of the young men from the craftsmen's valley, who lifted heavy stones and hammers all day.

Eskie nodded for Mando to be ready and raised his fist high to signal to Dubo and Dagan. He nudged Mando to get into position at the catwalk.

The youngster ambled toward the gate, with Jozman's basalt garden hoe hoisted on his shoulder. He carried one of the king's own guard's spear parallel to the ground.

Eskie leaned forward, feet spread, ready to spring into action. This had to work. *If there is help up above, I need it now, sir.*

"Gentlemen! We have ten contenders for the prize! Please take your places … and let the fights begin!"

* * *

Raucous cheering erupted.

Eskie dropped his arm.

Mando ducked under the stairway, out of sight from those above the gate with the king.

Hesitating only a moment, Eskie unsheathed his dagger and charged toward the stairs. He made as much clatter as he could with his feet and scraped his short sword along the stacked-stone wall.

Turning to the noise inside the city wall, the king's guards eyed Eskie's approach. The right-hand guard descended the steps in a run—a long sword in hand. He glared with menacing eyes, nostrils flared. Taking a backswing to his right, the shield in his left hand flared out.

Bad form, man—just the advantage I need. Eskie lunged with a thrust to the Amorite's left, just under his ribcage.

Surprise flushed the man's eyes. The glare dimmed, turning to blankness. His sword tipped from his lifeless hand and stabbed the ground, toppling over, as his knees buckled.

Eskie grabbed the hilt as soon as it hit ground, and crouched—while crowd noise outside reached a fever pitch.

Mando held high Jozman's basalt garden hoe. The king's second guard lay face down, immobile, where he landed when he tripped over the spear inserted across the third step of the stairs. Just as planned. *Except we did not know we would have a spear handle to work with. Providence? Thank you, sir.*

On the bridge, Dagan held Zobar wedged against the wall with a forearm at his throat and an arm twisted behind his back—just as Sir Ghaleb the Hittite taught him in Gibeon. Dubo inserted a linen rag into the king's mouth.

Eskie gagged the new king's best palace guard—the only one left—where he cowered at the feet of the palace's eleven-harvests-old former dung carrier. Eskie tied the hands and feet.

On the bridge, Dubo brandished the sword that fell at his feet, a gift from Crabaw, the ambusher. He held his weapon ready for the kill, while Dagan tied the king's hands behind his back. Then he looped it around the king's scrawny neck.

The crowd noise subsided with, "Aw-w-w."

Eskie drew a deep breath. *"Squee-ee-yew!"*

His men turned his way. Eskie raised a thumb high.

Jozman's voice rang loud and clear: "Bring the victors to the center ring."

* * *

Eskie wiped the blood from his dagger on the rail of the stairs and on the inside of his sling-stone bag and sheathed it at his side. He grabbed the hilt of the bronze sword no longer needed by Zobar's right-hand man. Taking up the dead man's shield, he clasped the sword between thumb and forefinger and allowed the prize to sway, as he held it loose.

The gate swung wide, pulled by Dagan.

Eskie eased out, holding the champion's rewards aloft. He presented them to Jozman, with his back to the crowd.

Trying to regain regular breathing, the Amorite victors stood with disdain on their faces and hands on their hips. Sweat poured down their bare chests. They eyed him with suspicion.

Eskie grinned. *Perhaps you men did not expect such a difficult challenge? On another day, those young men would have massacred you.*

Jozman nodded and moved beside the first of Zobar's soldiers. He raised the man's left arm high and stared at Eskie. "Who cheers for the winner of ring number one?"

"Humph." The crowd gave little response.

Jozman glanced back at Eskie and raised his chin a whisker or two, then continued asking for a voice vote for each of the king's strongmen.

Eskie understood Jozman's silent question. He expected Jebus to present the prizes. That was the plan. *Change of plans.*

"The Lord handed Lachish over to Israel." JOSHUA 10:32

Chapter 14
Lachish Has Fallen

The Jebusites take possession of Jerusalem   *Day 8*

If, according to plan, Xander and Sanbar and six Jebusite timbermen would come out of the Hinnom … *about now.*

Jozman confirmed the fifth victor had no more crowd appeal than the others.

Eskie turned and faced the crowd. He waited for quiet, smiling to see his men and the Jebusites' best strongmen in place, at the back.

Jozman stepped to Eskie's side and spoke behind his hand, "Where is Jebus?"

Eskie handed the sword and shield to Jozman, with a slight bow. "His father was very ill, sir. No water or food for three days or more. Jebus is still with him in the palace garden."

"All right. We proceed anyway."

"Yes, sir."

Jozman raised his voice. "Gentlemen, this young man is Eschol of Gibeon. Let us hear what he has to say."

Eskie inserted two fingers in his mouth. *"Squee-ee-yew!"*

119

Murmurs rippled through the crowd, as two bands of three Jebusite timbermen arrived at the front of the crowd. Naqib and other Jebusite merchants with ropes over their shoulders sidled up to any of Zobar's soldiers among the crowd.

Mando came to Eskie's side.

Jozman nodded to the timbermen, who took up places behind each of Zobar's men at the victors' circles.

Eskie raised his voice. "King Zobar, and gentlemen of the peaceful surrounds of Jerusalem, for a long time, a pall has overlaid this noble mount. Evil has reigned here, and integrity has hung its head. But today I say ... No more! I bring charges of murder against the god Molech and the sign of the double gash!"

The crowd gasped.

The king's henchman tensed, and eyed each other. They darted their gazes left and right—seeing the timbermen with arms the size of a five-year-old sapling blocking their way out.

Jozman shouted, "Gentlemen, Eschol of Gibeon brings charges of murder. We will hear him out."

The crowd approved with full-throated cheers.

Eskie lifted Mando to the low wall surrounding the spring. He jabbed his arm toward the top of the hill across the bin-Hinnom. "Mando, what did you see on the backside of the Hill of Evil Counsel ... three days ago?"

Mando raised his shrill, young voice. "Sir, I found a fresh cut of the double gash ... slashed on a tree on the other side of that hill."

The crowd rumbled like a cook pot about to boil over.

"*Squee-ee-yew!* ... Where else have you seen the sign of the double gash?"

"On my friend's house. The kind, old gentleman who tended the king's garden. And I never saw the old man again."

"Is there any other place you saw the sign of the double gash?"

"Yes!"

"Where?"

"In Molech's room in the palace."

"Molech's room?"

"It is the king's private room. In it, he stores all the soldiers' weapons. The sign of the double gash is painted in tar over the fireplace."

The crowd, as one body, took offense with deep rumblings.

Dagan emerged from the main gate, leading Zobar with a rope around his neck. Dubo shuffled along, step by step, with the king, directing Zobar with a tug and a squeeze at his elbow.

"Mando, what else did you see three days ago on the Hill of Evil Counsel?"

"A bloody spear stuck in the ground and one sandal hanging in the tree."

"Anything else?" Eskie spoke to Mando and gestured to Sanbar to come forward.

"Yes, sir. A single scraped line in the dirt. The line went to the top of the hill, and we looked down on the burning garbage of Hinnom Valley."

"A scraped line? Where did the scraped line start?"

"At the oak tree with the double gash and the one sandal hanging there."

"Is this the sandal? Sanbar. Show us the shoe."

Sanbar held the footwear high and came to face the crowd next to Mando.

Eskie pointed. "Mando, is this the sandal you found hanging from that tree?"

"Yes, sir. It is, and it is almost new."

Eskie turned to the shoemaker. "Sanbar, did you make this sandal?"

Sanbar patted his chest twice with an open hand.

Each timberman grabbed a wrestler's right arm and bent it behind his back and gave him a knee from behind—forcing him to fall to his knees with a thump and a whimper.

One of the wrestling champions snarled, "You have no call to accuse us. We deny any knowledge or involvement."

Jozman raised his voice. "Men of integrity, … "

The timbermen acted on cue, grabbing the other arm of each of Zobar's men.

"… lift these wrestlers' left arms high again."

Caught off guard, the luckless winners had no time to resist.

Eskie pointed at a man in the front of the crowd. "Sir, where do you come from?"

"The Mt. of Olives—there." The man pointed across the Kidron Valley.

"Would you tell us what you see under each of these men's left arms?"

The neighbor nodded and stooped to peer at their hairy sockets—going from one man to the other. He straightened and rubbed his nose. "They all have a fingernail-length scar, like a double gash. A two-stroke branding at the base of his left arm, perhaps by the heated edge of a sword."

The crowd mumbled.

Eskie pointed to another observer on the third row. "Sir, where are you from?"

"I am from Nob, beyond the Mt. of Olives on the Kidron."

"Would you inspect the left arm of King Zobar?"

The man forced his way through the milling crowd and approached the king, unabashed.

Dubo forced the king's left arm up, and Dagan ripped the red robe at the sleeve.

"Same! And I will be the first to spit in your face." Turning to Eskie, the man demanded, "Whose sandal was it?"

"Sanbar?"

Sanbar waved the sandal he still held aloft. "Da vis-i-er."

"The vizier? The only wise and just man who worked in the palace?" The Nob resident's face flared with anger.

The crowd rumbled, like distant thunder building energy.

"Hang them!"

"Hanging is too good for them!"

"Use the rope."

Eskie put two fingers to his lips. *"Squee-ee-yew!"*

The crowd turned silent. Expectant.

Jozman, chief of maintenance and construction in Jerusalem, proclaimed. "Men, the tower of Molech ordered by Zobar for today's entertainment stands ready! Jebusite men of valor and all who love justice, escort these worthless murderers to the gallows."

Eskie sucked in a deep breath, as the crowd drained away to watch the spectacle of multiple hangings in bin-Hinnom Valley.

Mando held up the sword and shield. "Sir, who will claim the wrestler's prize?"

Eskie grinned. "I do not know, Boy-dough, but none of those scoundrels need them now. They belong to Jozman."

Dubo and Dagan drew near. Dagan clutched his fist to his chest.

"Good work, men. We can be proud the bowmaker is out of the dungeon and Zobar and his counterparts are getting what they deserve. Thanks for your help." Eskie glanced at Dagan, questioning his pale coloring…

"Eskie!"

Knowing cousin Lehab called him, Eskie puzzled. *What message should I send to Baba?* Turning to his cousin and Ya-yah', he knew he could not return to Gibeon now. *Would he? … Ever?* "Lehab. What did you think of the longest-day celebration? How did you fare in the archery contest?"

He shrugged. "I was third place for youth, but I will do better next year. Baba said I could trade Mamaa's hand-woven girdles for a Jebusite bow." He held it for Eskie to admire.

"Excellent bow, made by the masters at bow making. Next year you will win, no doubt."

"Is your friend Jebus well?"

"Jebus needs more time, but we freed his father from the king's dungeon today. Though he, too, is very ill."

"Your baba will be glad your reason for coming to Jerusalem is done. When will you come home?"

"I am ... not sure. I still have more to do here ... helping Jebus ... and all ..."

Ya-yah', standing behind Lehab, dipped his chin and narrowed his eyes.

"... But Dubo or Dagan may want to go back with you."

Dubo spoke up, "Yes. I need to go back and provide for my mother."

"Dagan?" Breaking eye contact with Ya-yah', Eskie shrugged a question.

Dagan set his feet wider, with his fists on his hips, and spat on the ground. "What do I have to go back to?" ...

Ya-yah' broke the silence. "Lehab, get our animals from the livery pen while I pack up."

Dagan gruffed, "I will go with him."

Eskie turned back to Ya-yah's penetrating stare. "Tell Baba I will return to Gibeon soon, but, for now, I cannot ... yet."

* * *

Standing between the two Jebusite leaders at Jerusalem's main gate, Eskie crossed his arms at his chest. Across the Hinnom on the tower of Molech, six bodies swayed in the breeze. The market-day crowd milled about the spring, munching stuffed grape leaves, their mood much improved.

"Gentlemen, it was an honor to serve you. I am ready to return to Nephtoah. Perhaps to Gibeon in a few days, but I have a question about Mando. Does he have any family left in Jerusalem that he can return to?"

Jozman bit his lip a moment. "No, he does not. In fact, one of the first things I must do is provide food and shelter for the orphans and widows of Zedek's army, or we will have a dire situation on our hands very soon."

"Sir, I like Mando's attitude, and we work well together. I would offer to provide for him as long as he needs me."

"That would be kind of you."

"And the thing I do best back at home is to go hunting and to provide extra meat for the cooks. I will see what I can do in the next few days to help feed the widows and the orphans here."

Naqib, chief of the Jebusite clan, lowered his voice. "Gentlemen, we must not forget the threat of the Hebrews, as well. How can we take over occupying Jerusalem and avoid a battle with the Hebrews, who far outnumber us?"

At the edge of the area of the Gihon Spring, a young man appeared from the depth of the Kidron valley, ready to collapse. "Where is the king ... of Jerusalem?"

"Meanwhile, Horam king of Gezer had come up to help Lachish, but Joshua defeated him and his army—until no survivors were left." JOSHUA 10:33

Chapter 15
Brothers

On the way to Nephtoah   *Day 8*

With sundown colors painting the sky, Eskie and his band of men, shrunk now to only three, ambled along the rocky path to the waters of Nephtoah.

He smiled, pleased with the accomplishment of the day. Where did his own words come from when he addressed the crowd at Gihon Spring? *God Most High? Star Namer? Ruler over the white owl?*

"Sir?"

"Mando?"

"Mr. Jozman said I am to stay with you now."

"Yes. I asked Jozman if you had kin you could go back to in Jerusalem. When he said no, I asked him to let me be responsible for you. Is that agreeable to you?"

"Am I your slave now?"

Eskie flinched and stopped, placing a hand on his friend's

shoulder. "No, Mando. More like my little brother for as long as you need me."

Mando's eyebrows shot up, and he grabbed Eskie around the waist.

Eskie tousled Mando's shock of unkempt hair. The boy sobbed.

Dagan looked away, stone-faced. Surprised by his own emotions, Eskie rubbed his nose with the back of his fist. "Men, here and now, I pledge to both of you, you are adopted into the Ra-eef' clan for as long as you choose to be a part of my family. From here on out, we are brothers, together."

Mando dropped his arms and stepped back with tear-stained cheeks. "Forever, sir?"

"Yes, Mando. So you do not have to call me 'sir' ever again. I am Eskie."

Trapped again with Mando at his waist, Eskie grinned at Dagan and pried Mando off a little. He extended his hand, palm up, waist high. "From here on out, Dagan. Brothers?"

Mando's small hand topped Eskie's.

Dagan drew back, right fist pressing his stomach, and jeered, "You do not want an Amorite for a brother. Maybe I do not want a Gibeonite, either."

Eskie topped Mando's hand and bounced the stack—shocked by Dagan's boiling-angry eyes.

Eskie cleared his throat. "Men, it is a very good thing this is the longest *natural* day of the year. But we should pick up the pace if we want to arrive at Nephtoah before midnight. I am hoping Miss 'Zalef has something saved for us. I could eat a bear."

"Me, too!" Mando rubbed his belly.

Cold stew would be just fine, but warm would be even better. ... We shall see. ... But what can I do about Dagan? He is so angry and bitter.

కుఖ

Keshub cringed and rubbed his nose. He and the son of the high priest and the ten Levites neared another battlefield burn pile, still smoldering. At the bottom of the hill, a small village teemed with activity.

Mr. Phinehas quickened his step at the sight. He hailed the first man they came to. "Where is Ocran the Naphtalite, sir?"

"Mr. Phinehas! I will find him for you." The man hurried away to the village.

Eskie pointed. "Sir, I see a spring and a pool yonder. May I refill your flask?"

"Yes, please." He drained the clay juglet and handed it to Keshub.

On the way, Keshub passed packs for donkeys lined up in the shade under trees beside the path. He helped Uncle Yaakoub many times in the last few moons with similar gear.

Returning with juglets full of water, Keshub identified bags of grain and dried fruits, a bag of fresh melons and another of leeks. *These spoils of war must be ready to go to either Joshua and the army or back to Gilgal. If to Joshua, maybe I can travel with them.*

Keshub stopped near Mr. Phinehas, waiting to give him his flask. The high priest's son spoke with two Hebrew men from among the cleanup crew.

"Ocran, your tribe of Naphtalites has done excellent work here. I smell no stench. I commend you and your men. We would not want the Promised Land to be defiled by disease and decay. You will be rewarded for your diligence in this difficult task."

Mr. Phinehas reached for his full juglet. "Amned, this is Keshub, our guide from Gilgal and Joshua's aide. He would like to travel with you Asherites taking supplies to Joshua tomorrow."

The leader of the battlefield-acquisition-and-supply-transport team lowered his brows and eyed Keshub. "He is very young."

Mr. Phinehas' face cracked with a rare smile. "Yes, he is, but he is mature for his age."

"The Asherites leave from the spring at first light—before the sun rises."

"He will be ready. I am sure. Right, Keshub?"

"Yes, sir. I will report to the spring at the second watch to help water the donkeys before loading up."

Mr. Amned pursed his lips and nodded.

* * *

Early morning on the trail to Lachish   *Day 9*
with the Asherite supply train

Keshub imagined Uncle Yaakoub led the donkeys ahead, while he traipsed along behind—Raja at his side loaded with Ra-eef' pottery. But no. Those days passed not so long ago. This donkey belonged to the Hebrews, acquired after the battle of Makkedah. Probably older than Raja, she favored her right front hoof. He must examine Mak's hoof at the first stop along the way.

A finger under her girth strap and bridle before they started out seemed all right. But he wished her breast strap had more padding for the uphill parts of the journey. He must ask about that at the first stop, too. He was glad going uphill in the low hills of this region did not compare with the steepness of the climb from Jericho to the ridgeline trail.

Keeping pace, he took up the slack in the lead rope with one hand and laid a cautious hand on Mak's shoulder. She did not reject him. The muscles flexed rhythmically with each step.

ῴῳ

In the Rephaim forest   *Day 9*

Eskie kept his voice low. "Men, we will walk single file. I am scouting for signs of wild goats or deer to show you. A hoof print or a dropping. A trail or a skittering in the undergrowth. We will make a marker to come back to. Two flat stones stacked like this—and one beside them, pointing to the way we came. But not too obvious. Tucked away a bit. Remember the surroundings. The stones will confirm.

"Remember this when you go out alone. After every several paces, make for yourself another marker within sight, pointing back to the first one. Remember: two stacked stones with one beside them, pointing back to the last marker. You can follow your markers back to where we started together. Understand?"

Eskie sensed uneasiness in their eyes. Mando had never been in the forest before, and certainly not hunting. He made his tone lighter. "We would not want anyone to get lost. Then we would have to scare off all the game, while we searched for our lost brother. Right? We will not hunt alone—always at least two of us together. Understood? Follow me."

"Sir, in only a few days, I have come from knowing nothing about you to cautiously believing you are watching over what is happening down here. The white owl showed me maybe you are watching over me, too? Please help me lead my adopted brothers, who have had no father or only a bad father in their lives. Dagan certainly needs a friend, even if he does not want a brother."

෫෬

Taking a break on the trail to Lachish to join Joshua

Keshub hobbled Mak, with his girdle tied between her forelegs, before he took a quick gulp from his flask. He snatched a handful of bunchgrass from beside the trail and laid it on the ground at Mak's feet. While she munched, he checked her girth strap and tightened it.

Her breast-strap padding concerned him. He inserted a blade of grass in his mouth and waved at his trail leader, Mr. Amned. He would ask him for help. While he waited, he gave Mak more grass.

"Sir?" Keshub hailed the trail leader, as he came near, checking each donkey and its handler.

"What do you need, young man? Remind me of your name."

"Keshub, sir. Joshua's Gibeonite slave."

"Ah, yes. What do you need?"

Keshub showed him the thinnish breast piece of the pack. "Sir, I wonder if we have anything we can add here to soften the chafing on the uphill treks."

Mr. Amned tilted his head. "You have done this before, I see."

"Yes, sir. And I need your help to lift Mak's right front foot. She seems to be favoring it."

"All right. Let's see if there is a problem."

"I will hold her steady, while you look, sir."

"Thank you. You have a good hobble here, but you might need your girdle again. I will see if we can find you a short rope for next time."

"Yes, sir. Thank you."

"You are right, Keshub. There is a small stone wedged behind her hoof. What did you say her name is?"

"Oh, sorry, sir. I call her Mak because she is from Makkedah. I had a favorite donkey back in Gibeon named Raja. She was a good companion on the long trail between Jericho and Gibeon."

"I see. That is how you know about needing the extra padding in front."

"Yes, sir."

"All right. See me tonight to get some ointment to put on Mak's hoof, and I may need you to help with inspecting the packs tomorrow. Maybe then we can get on the trail sooner."

"Yes, sir."

☙◊❧

In the forest of Rephaim

Twilight in the forest comes early on the sunset side of this valley. Eskie chided himself for not starting back to Nephtoah sooner and not setting trail signs closer together. Already the dusk made markers difficult to see. Starlight and the waning moon would be no help if they did not make it back to the spring soon.

"Ez-gee."

Eskie's insides nearly jumped out of his skin. He knew who called his name but had no idea Reef could be nearby. "Reef? Is that you?"

"Yez." His deep voice rumbled. "There'z an easier trail thiz way. Follow me."

"Thanks, man. This certainly is a rugged valley. Have you lived here all your life?"

"Yez. The valley iz known for my family. Most people are afraid of thiz valley because of us, but we are not like the sonz of Anak over at Hebron. Those big fellows are mean. They would rather fight than eat, I think."

Eskie chuckled. "Man, could you help us tomorrow? We need two or three more kills to take to Jerusalem. There are a lot of widows and orphans there, without their menfolk to provide for them. Zedek took every available man to the battle of Gibeon."

"Lots of widows?"

"Yes, that is right. Maybe you can find a wife there. Do you want me to ask around for you?"

Reef scratched the back of his head. "Would you? We need five."

"You need five wives?"

"No. For my brothers, two cousins, and me."

"Sure. I will ask. All they can say is yes or no."

"Um-hum. That is what I am afraid of. Thiz iz the way back. Just a little farther, and you will have sunlight for the rest of the way to Nephtoah."

While the others caught up with him, Eskie stopped and changed the hand dragging the little doe ibex tied to a sapling behind him. Next came Mando pulling their knapsacks lashed to two smaller branches. Farther back, Dagan, breathing too hard, dragged another ibex on a sapling.

"Reef, can you hunt with me again tomorrow? The others will smoke this meat tomorrow, and we will take the fresh and the smoked to Jerusalem the next day. I will tell of your proposal then and see what they say.

"Come this way at first light. I will be here—if pa does not need me."

"Then Joshua … moved on from Lachish to Eglon. They took up positions against it and attacked it. They captured it that same day and put it to the sword and totally destroyed everyone in it, just as they had done to Lachish." JOSHUA 10:34-35

Chapter 16
The Jebusites Take Charge

On the road to Lachish with the Asherite supply train   *Day 10*

"The Lachish cleanup crew says Joshua moved on to Eglon last night and will destroy it today. We have new orders. Joshua said we are to change directions and bypass Lachish. We join Joshua at Eglon tonight."

Keshub ducked his head. He could not help overhearing the Asherite scout report to Amned, leader of the supply train.

* * *

He topped every hill with butterflies in his stomach, hoping to see Joshua and his army down below. Disappointed again, Keshub picked up a stone. Shrugging to loosen his shoulders, he chose a target a stone's throw away. He wound up with his best imitation of his brother Eskie the marksman and hurled with all his might. "Thwack."

"Shu-ree." The handler behind him whistled encouragement.

Keshub waved his thanks and doubled his stride to catch up with his donkey. "Mak, I am glad we found extra padding for your front gear. We are not in the easy hills of the shephelah anymore, since we angled back toward Jerusalem today. Baba said Eskie took Jebus back to Jerusalem. Surely when Joshua heads back to Gilgal, he must go to Jerusalem. Will Joshua attack Jerusalem, too?" *Will Eskie be caught in the crossfire?*

சி

Delivering game to Jerusalem   *Day 11*

Eskie checked his donkey's cinch. "Dagan, I   need to talk to Mr. Jozman after we make our delivery. Would you and Mando take the donkeys to the liveryman? Mando, you know where he is, right?"

"Yes, sir. … I mean, yes, brother. I know the way." Mando waggled his head.

Eskie smirked. "When you get there, offer to help him with his work in return, and I will bring something from the delivery to add to his supper. Can you do that?"

Dagan scowled. "What will we have to do?"

"Easy stuff. Like forking hay in the troughs, raking up dung, or filling water troughs. You should offer to chop wood, too. Just make yourselves useful. I do not know how long I will be."

Passing the dung gate and two pine trees, Eskie looked for the gallows in the Hinnom Valley on the other side of the road. In its place, a pile of split firewood stood ready … to smoke game perhaps? *I think Jozman is expecting us.*

At the main gate, two burly young Jebusites guarded the entrance. "Good morning, men. I have wild game to take to Mr.

Jozman. Can you direct us to him?"

"He is usually at the palace by this time. What do you have?"

"A deer and three ibexes."

"That will make a big difference. All the widows and orphans are being moved to the palace today. Jozman is organizing their care. You are the Gibeonite from market day, right?"

"Yes. We are both from Gibeon. I am Eskie, son of the potter. This is … Dagan."

The guard glanced at Dagan and back to Eskie.

"Perhaps you know Mando. He is from here, but he is with me now. Mando can take us to the kitchen and find Mr. Jozman. Right, Mando?"

"Yes, sir. Follow me!"

* * *

"Eskie! You had good hunting, I am told." Jozman waved him into a room near the kitchen.

"Yes, sir. The kitchen staff has the delivery and is already preparing to smoke most of it. They seemed excited."

"I am sure. A kitchen with nothing to cook is a sad tale, indeed. And we have many mouths to feed. We will make this last as long as possible. The bean and melon crops are producing well, and wheat harvest was good here. Can you bring us more in a few days? We are regathering our flocks that were neglected and scattered while Zobar dithered with staying in power. Did Gibeon's farmers get their wheat in before the battle?"

"Yes, sir, they did. The day before the battle all hands were in the fields. We did not know *if* we would survive to eat it, but we knew *if we survived* the battle we would not live out the year with no wheat."

"Jerusalem has always counted on buying wheat from Aijalon Valley farmers."

"Yes, sir. On a different subject, I have a proposition for you."

"Oh?"

"Yes, from one of the Rephaim brothers, who works for Za'atar."

"All right. What is his proposition?"

"He needs a wife."

"A wife?"

"Yes, I mentioned the wild game would help feed the widows and the orphans in Jerusalem. He would like to offer a home to as many as five of your widows and their children."

"Five?"

"He has two brothers and two cousins."

Jozman shrugged. "I can ask. All they can say is yes or no."

"That is what I said."

"Are there any terms?"

"No. I think the women can set their own terms, perhaps."

"I will tell the women of your offer and see what happens. Have you heard the latest about the Hebrews? The king of Gezer came down to help Lachish on the day after Lachish was overrun. The Hebrews routed Horam's army and yesterday were moving this direction. Probably going to Eglon next, but definitely coming this way."

Eskie shook his head. "What about Hebron? Do you think that city can stop the Hebrews?"

"I do not know, but Hebron sits on the highest ground in Canaan. And they have the advantage of the sons of Anak among their army. They are big and fierce fighters, but, right now, the Hebrews appear to be invincible." Jozman tented his fingers at his chin over his short beard.

Eskie counted on his fingers. "Two days from now, I would expect them to observe their Sabbath again. Even if they come straight here, that would give us at least four or five days before they could arrive at Jerusalem. But surely a battle with Hebron would take longer than a day. Right?"

Jozman shrugged. "How did Gibeon avoid a battle and get a treaty?"

"Gibeon was saved from destruction by the faith of one man, my father, the potter. For many years, he wanted to know more about an all-knowing god of the heavens, who named the stars. When Baba realized an all-powerful god fought the Hebrews' battles, he wanted to know more."

"What do you mean?"

"Baba had refused an alliance with Zedek and his Molech god twice. He knew no god made by the hands of men has power to help—or hinder. He says those gods are only the devices of evil men to hold power over others."

"Your father refused Zedek twice? He is a man of wisdom and great courage."

"That he is. I spied from the cliff above Jericho, when the Hebrews crossed the Jordan River on dry ground. I shook with the earthquake, when their priests stepped one foot into the wide, rushing waters."

"You were there?"

"I perched on the ridge above Jericho from only a few days after the longest night six new moons ago. ... Before the Jordan flooded and became impossible to cross. I kept asking 'What ... are ... they ... waiting ... for?'"

"Did you see Jericho fall?"

"I did. All the Hebrews did was march around Jericho, slowly, with rams' horns blaring—once, for six days. By that time, we were sending a Gibeonite spy home to report every day."

"Zedek did the same here."

"Yes. We all knew an attack would happen soon. I am sure we were all asking, 'What ... are ... they ... waiting ... for?' The day they marched around Jerusalem seven times and shouted, the walls fell outward. Joshua's army walked straight in on a ramp of fallen bricks."

"Amazing."

"Yes, sir, it was. I jogged home on that moonless night, on that treacherous, narrow trail." Eskie swallowed. "Lit by the fire of Jericho's destruction. Baba thought then the Hebrews were unbeatable, but the battle at Ai changed his mind. Baba said the Hebrew god is not like men. Baba saw a chance to survive when no one else did."

"How is that?"

"The Hebrews were defeated the first time at Ai. Remember?"

"Yes. Do you know why?"

"My father says their all-powerful god fought for them as they crossed the flooded river and at the battle of Jericho. But their god did not help them at Ai. They were on their own."

"Why not?"

"We do not know why, but, the next day, a man and his whole family were executed outside the Hebrew camp at Gilgal by public stoning. Their god was not happy about something. Baba decided the only way for Gibeon to survive was to ask for a treaty and to see what happened. He led a delegation to Gilgal and took a risk he would be killed immediately. He was determined to save his family and community from destruction. But also because he wanted to learn more about the god who cares for his chosen people—and disciplines them like a father."

Jozman drew a deep breath. "The chosen people. That makes the rest of us the unchosen."

"Right you are, but the white owl that sits in a pine tree at the dung gate has shown me that maybe the real god of the Hebrews cares about the unchosen, too. And, now that I think of it, maybe the Hebrews were waiting all those days for orders from their god. Maybe their god made them wait so we could bring in the wheat harvest."

Jozman stared. "A god who cares?"

Eskie shrugged.

"So how do we translate these thoughts and questions into a plan for Jerusalem? Do we have a chance to survive?"

"That ... is the question."

* * *

Eskie swung a coarse linen bag filled with smoked ibex, as he approached the livery pen. "Hallow! Look what I brought for your supper."

The liveryman rose from his work bench, piled high on one end with bridles and other gear. "Eskie!"

"Good day to you, sir. Did Dagan and Mando help out today?"

"Yes, good workers. Because you sent them, I almost caught up on my saddlery repairs. And one or the other played goats' knuckles with my son most of the time. He is always in such pain it was good for him to have something else to think about today. Say, is the younger one a Zedek offspring?"

"Yes, he is. A cast-off grandson, he said, but he is with me now. I adopted him."

"Adopted?"

"Yes. We have become like brothers, and he is a great help to me. There are so many widows and orphans in the city Mr. Jozman is taking care of them in the palace. I brought venison and ibex today to help feed them."

"Many changes around here since Zedek left. Mostly for the better."

Eskie nodded. "I need to start back to Nephtoah. We will see you again soon, I am sure. Thanks for the livery today."

"Certainly."

Turning away, Eskie puzzled. *Who does that man sound like? His voice seems so familiar.*

* * *

"Dagan, how was your work with the liveryman?"

"Good."

"Glad to hear it. Did he keep you busy?"

"Mostly. But I also played goats' knuckles in the shade with his son for a while."

"How is the son?"

"In pain, most of the time. He cannot walk. He has to crawl. His baba asked me to come back to help on market day five days from now. He said I was good with the animals. Do you think I can?"

"Of course. If you like working with the animals, I think it is a great opportunity for you." *That is the first actual conversation I have had with Dagan. Maybe there is hope for this young man.*

"[Joshua] *went up from Eglon.*" JOSHUA 10:36

Chapter 17
Lost

In the forest of Rephaim west of Jerusalem   *Day 12*

"Ez-gee."

Eskie startled. "Wha-a?" *How does he do that? Big man, big feet. How can he be so silent in the forest?*

"What did they say?"

"Who?"

Reef gulped. "The widows."

"Oh, that. I did not talk face to face with the women. I gave your proposition to Jozman. He has the task of providing for the widows, and he said he would ask—said they could only say yes or no—just like I told you."

The big fellow appeared to droop like a flower wilting before Eskie's eyes.

He reached a hand to the big man's shoulder. "These things take time, Reef. The women are grieving over husbands and sons right now. I am sure Jozman will make your offer soon, but it is a big decision. They may need to think about it for a while before they answer."

"How long?"

"Man, who knows? We must be patient. In the meantime, all I know to do is keep them busy in the kitchen. We are helping so they have no time to worry about where the next meal will come from—for themselves and for their children.

"All right. We have to wait."

"And ... go hunting."

ဢဢ

Preparation day for Sabbath with Joshua's army

Keshub laid tinder and kindling for a small fire at first light. Would he ever awaken before his master?

Joshua knelt, praying, a stone's throw away.

Keshub rasped his flint and iron together. A spray of sparks landed on the spider web he found last night, before the dew appeared. Joshua looked so different. Shaggy hair and beard. Deep creases in his forehead and leathery skin, from so many days in the sun. Twelve straight days trekking from battle to battle—did he eat a sit-down meal in that time? Please help him get some rest today, Lord.

"Good morning." Joshua stretched his arms wide and rolled his shoulders.

"Yes, sir, it is. The forest is a great place to prepare for the Sabbath rest. I will have a rosemary tea for you soon. The water is heating."

Joshua rubbed his hands over his face and beard. "Thank you for bringing me a change of clothes and the sandals. It is hard to think how our sandals did not wear out the whole time we were in the wilderness. Now we are in the Promised Land less than three months, and these sandals I have worn for over forty years are falling apart. The Promised Land is also the real world."

"Yes, sir."

"I am going to the spring."

* * *

Keshub used a forked branch and the end of his girdle to grasp the hot cooking pot below the rim. Removing it from the fire, he covered the pot of lentil stew with a flat rock. He banked the coals for later. The Asherite camp cooks would supply roasted meat and bread.

He emptied his knapsack and slouched it over his shoulder. Fresh greens or fruit from the forest would be perfect to go with the Sabbath day cold lentil stew.

* * *

Deep in the forest, Keshub grabbed his knapsack full of fresh figs and mallow leaves. He would provide Joshua a Sabbath feast at dusk that Mamaa Danya would be proud of.

He stopped. "Now … which way do I go?" He swallowed the sudden lump in his throat. He should not have come alone. … He should have laid more trail markers, as Eskie had taught him. … He should not have come this far—out of sight of the camp. … He should have… "But stop. Here I am. I do not know what to do next or where to turn. … I am all alone …" He cleared his throat and spoke louder. "Except for God Most High. … Talking aloud in this dense forest … I will pray to the only one who can hear me.

"Lord, you know my *heretofore* and you know my *hereafter*. God Most High, you named the stars. You watched over us when Baba got the crazy idea to dress in rags and worn-out sandals."

Snap.

Keshub prayed even louder. "Lord, you are God Most High, watching over us all. You know how I got here, and you can lead me back. Forgive me for my willful pride that got me lost—"

"Keshub! Is that you?"

"Eskie?"

"Man, how did you get here?"

"I was foraging for my supper. I must have strayed too far, and I went around the fig tree several times." *Slow down and do not sound panicked. After all, I am ten plus three harvests old now.*

He sucked in a calming breath. "Then I forgot which way I came from, and now in the forest shadows, I cannot tell from the sun which way to go. I was praying God Most High would show me the way like he promised the Hebrews' Father Abraham. ... And you showed up, big brother."

Eskie hesitated then smirked. "Well, you were praying so loud someone was sure to come. It just happened to be me. So you are with Joshua again?"

"Yes. Are you here by yourself, too? Baba said you took Jebus back to Jerusalem to free his father from the dungeon. How did that go?"

"It went well—with a whole bunch of help from a scary, old, white owl and whoever tells him to sit there and hoot at just the right moment. We freed Jebus's father, and exposed Zedek and his son, Zobar, as murdering thugs. And get this: the Jebusites hanged the king and his henchmen on the tower of Molech that day."

"Whoa. What are you doing here today?"

"Hunting to take meat back to Jerusalem. Mr. Jozman, one of the Jebusite leaders, has all the widows and orphans of Zedek's army housed in the king's palace. He is providing for them there. How is that for justice? Zedek's palace of evil replaced by a home for the destitute and starving?"

"Truly amazing. But I should go back. Can you point me the way out of the forest toward ... the Negev?"

"That way. "

"Thanks, big brother. I think the One who directed your white owl directed your steps today to help me out of big trouble." Keshub grabbed Eskie and clung tight. "Until we meet again, brother."

Keshub waved good-bye. *Lord, please do not allow us to face each other on opposite sides in a battle for Jerusalem.*

☙◊❧

Eskie clapped Keshub on the back and watched him disappear into thick foliage of low-hanging branches. "Take care little brother." …

"Ez-gee."

Eskie rejoined Reef on the other side of a dense grove of oak saplings.

"I heard you talking. Is your brother with the enemy of Canaan?"

Eskie winced and shrugged. "He is slave to Joshua, leader of the Hebrews. Let's head back, and I will tell you how all that happened. And I assure you the wise men of the Jebusites are seeking a way to avoid a battle with them. We will see how that works out." *God Most High, is there a way to avoid a battle with the Hebrews? Baba found a way for the Gibeonites. Can the Jebusites survive too?*

☙◊❧

Back in Joshua's camp

"Keshub, I was getting concerned. It will be sundown soon and the beginning of Sabbath."

"I am so sorry, sir. I thought I would only go a little way, but I think I got lost when I went all around a fig tree, picking the ripe fruit." He held up his bulging knapsack. "I lost sight of which direction I came from. When I realized I was lost, I prayed aloud, mostly to calm my fears, and asked God to help me. And he sent my big brother, Eskie."

"Why was he in the forest of the Rephaim?"

Keshub took four figs from his knapsack. "He was hunting for game to feed the widows and orphans in Jerusalem. They are living in Zedek's palace. The Jebusites took over there last week and hanged the son of Zedek on the contraption built for Molech's fire. Would you like a fig?"

Joshua nodded. "Sounds good. What did you tell your brother about our camp?"

Keshub wrinkled his face. "I tried not to tell him anything. I asked him which way to go to get back to the Negev."

"That is probably the best you could do under the circumstances. You did not choose to escape from being my slave. Why?"

Keshub thought a moment, while he palmed four figs and poured water over them. He rolled and rubbed them with both hands before he extended the largest two figs and met Joshua's eyes. "Sir, my father gave his word. And you kept your word and defended Gibeon, when we were attacked. I could do no less …"

Keshub smiled. "And I would hear no more of your stories on the Sabbath about how God Most High has led his chosen people for these many years. Those stories gave my gran-mamaa comfort through the night on the day the sun stood still. She struggled for every breath, but she passed with a smile on her face, as the sun came up the next morning."

"I see." Joshua took a bite and recovered a bit of juice on his lip. "Good fig."

Keshub slurped, too. "May I tell you about Jebus and Eskie and why Eskie went to Jerusalem after the battle in Aijalon Valley?"

Joshua nodded. "I would like to hear it."

"Sir, it all started on the day Moses went up on Mount Nebo."

"How could that be?"

ജയങ

"Eskie?"

He twisted his head toward the soft voice speaking his name at twilight. "Yes. Do you need something?" Except for giving him the pickled duck's egg on market day, Pickle Girl had never before approached him.

"I have a question."

Eskie swiveled toward her on the log stool in her family's court-yard. "You have a question about … ?" The pulse sounding in his ears joined the chorus of bull frogs in the pond.

"About Dagan."

"Has he been misbehaving or slacking while I was away hunt-ing?"

"No, but I am worried about him?"

"Worried?"

"Yes. I think he is not well."

"What do you think is wrong with him?"

"I do not know. He tries not to let it show, but I believe he is in pain."

Eskie tilted his head. Her dark eyes sparkled with light reflected from the evening's fire.

"He clutches his chest sometimes, and he groans when he thinks no one will hear. And … I think he is worse today."

Eskie nodded. "I have seen and heard both without thinking more about it, since I have not seen blood."

'Zalef clutched her honey-colored head wrap at her chin. "I think this is something inside of him, not a cut or wound."

"Do you have any ideas of what we can do to help him?"

She broke her gaze and cast her eyes downward. "At the least, I think he should rest. He should not be chopping wood. Sleep would be best. Then he would not be aggravating his injury, if that is what it is. Then we must wait and see. You should tell him this."

Her eyes wide and imploring again, "My younger brother died at about Dagan's age. He was kicked in the chest by a donkey." She turned and fled, with her golden shawl picking up the last of twi-light, as she glided to the house.

Eskie's shoulders slumped. "'A donkey kicked him in the chest.' That certainly describes Dagan's father." Eskie witnessed Ragar's powerful fist to Dagan's stomach back at the wood camp. *Dagan's life may be in danger, sir. You are the all-powerful god of the Hebrews.*

I surely can be nothing in your sight. But it surely seemed like you used a white owl and me to rescue Jebus's father. And then ... freeing Jerusalem of Zobar—something I did not have in mind to do. Did ... you use me to answer Keshub's prayer today when he was lost? ... Would you help me with a young man who is abused and neglected by his father?

"[Sabbath day of rest.]" JOSHUA 10:36

Chapter 18
Dagan and the Liveryman

Another delivery to Jerusalem   *Day 13*

"Eskie!"

"Jebus!" Eskie, engulfed by Jebus's strong arms, wheezed out. "You are surely better. How is your vision?"

"Splendid! And hitting the mark again. Seeing double had me quite concerned for a while."

"I am sure. And how is your father?"

Jebus sobered. "He is better, but not well. I hear you are bringing wild game to the palace about every two days."

"Yes. I brought another delivery today with the help of Mando. The Rephaim brothers have helped with the hunting in their valley. I am on my way to speak to Jozman now."

"Perhaps I can join you."

* * *

"Eskie, I was expecting a visit from you. The kitchen staff said you brought them more work to do." Jozman smiled and rose from his cushioned position at the reed mat. He clasped Eskie by the shoulders for a cheek-to-cheek … then the same for his nephew, Jebus. "Sit with me."

"Am I bringing too much or too often?" Eskie folded his legs beneath him.

"No, no. They are delighted, and they are being miserly with all you have brought. They are smoking or drying as much as possible, to save it for later. But stew, even with a little meat, is a treat. Our youngsters are rosy-cheeked and healthy for the first time in a long while."

"Have you spoken to the women about the proposal from the Rephaim brothers?"

"Yes, but no response yet. We had news from Hebron yesterday."

"What is happening there?" Eskie pursed his lips.

"One of our men was there for market day. He said market day was slow, because their army had moved out early to help defend Debir from the Hebrews. I expect to hear a battle report sometime …"

Eskie interrupted. "But remember: today is the Hebrew Sabbath day of rest. Their god commands it. I met my little brother, lost in the Rephaim forest yesterday at midday."

"Keshub?" Jebus frowned. "Is he with Joshua and the Hebrews again?"

"Yes. He is Joshua's slave."

Jozman dipped his chin and angled his gaze at Eskie. "I would like to hear more about that, but why was he in the Rephaim forest?"

"He was foraging for figs and mallow greens to go with cold stew on the Sabbath, since they are not allowed to cook on the Sabbath. Their god commands that, too."

Jebus stiff-armed his hands to his knees. "Your brother was a long way from Debir."

"Yes, he was." Eskie tilted his head and squinted. "Keshub asked me to point him to the Negev … but maybe … "

"What are you thinking?" Jebus lowered his brow.

Eskie scratched the back of his head. "The Hebrews … defeated Eglon two days ago, right?"

"Yes. That is what we were told." Jebus exchanged glances with Jozman.

"Everybody expected them to be at Debir yesterday. That is the next walled city in line with the others they fought at the battle of Gibeon. Right?"

"Ye-es."

"Your man said Hebron's army went to help Debir defeat the Hebrews. Right?"

"Yes."

"But what if the Hebrews, instead of going near Debir, went to the Rephaim ridge and were hiding among the trees, preparing for their Sabbath day's rest?"

Jozman leaned forward. "So you are saying Hebron's army is in Debir, but there is no battle …"

Jebus interrupted, "Because there are no Hebrews there."

Eskie threw back his head and laughed. "Yes! I know the Hebrews are not there because they do not work or fight on the Sabbath. But if the Hebrews are observing the movements of Hebron, where will the Hebrews go as soon as the Sabbath is finished?"

Jozman and Jebus said, together, "To Hebron?"

"It is brilliant." Eskie's smile faded, as he saw the horror on the faces of the two Jebusites before him.

Jebus leveled his gaze. "Eskie, if they defeat Hebron tomorrow, which they might very well do, the Hebrews could be crossing the Kidron on the next day."

"Oh. … Yes, there is that."

Across the floor mat, Jozman hung his head and massaged his temples. "So the question is, gentlemen, how do we defend Jerusalem from a far-superior army ... in two days?"

"Sir, let's think about this." Eskie called on his many long talks with Sir Ghaleb, the Hittite soldier. "They have far superior numbers, but what about their weapons and their marksmen?"

"What do you mean?" Jebus reached out and clasped Eskie's forearm.

"When planning our strategy, we must look at their advantage, of course, but we must not forget to consider the Jebusites' strengths."

"For strengths, my father's bows and my uncle's arrows are far superior to any I have ever used. And many caravanners have said the same." Jebus stroked his beard and twisted his mouth. "Baba also had a special project he was working on before Zedek put him in the dungeon."

Jozman lowered his chin and directed a sidewise glance at Jebus.

Jebus cleared his throat. "Eskie, how would you rate the Hebrews' weapons?"

Eskie sensed their wariness to reveal the bowmaker's special project. He could not blame them. "Sir, I watched the Hebrews circle Jericho every day for seven days. I was impressed by their lack of weaponry made for war—except for the first unit, which, apparently, always leads them into battle."

Jebus turned sideways and gave Eskie his full attention. "What was different about the lead unit?"

"I talked to Sir Ghaleb. He is the old Hittite soldier in Gibeon who trains our young men to defend Gibeon. Their weapons, according to him, were most likely seized after their battles with Sihon of Heshbon and with Og of Bashan."

Jozman dipped his chin. "We had all believed those two would surely defeat the Hebrews on the other side of the Jordan. Even after Sihon fell at Jazer, we were confident Og and his giant sons and their vast army would stop them. Our strengths are the valleys on three sides of Mount Moriah, the wall around the city, and Gihon Spring. Zedek took almost all weapons with him to the battle at Gibeon."

Jebus numbered off on one hand. "The tally for the Hebrews is this. They far outnumber us, and they have doggedly put to the sword our allies, with victories over Gezer, Makkedah, Libnah, and Eglon. Debir and Hebron are left."

Jozman closed his eyes and shook his head. "When you put it that way, we are almost surrounded, and we are on the Hebrews' path to Gilgal, where their families wait for their return."

Eskie spoke just above a whisper. "And they worship a god who stopped the midday sun from going down about a whole day."

...

* * *

Eskie whistled as he neared the livery. *"Squee-ee-yew."*

Mando came running. "Whoa. You stayed a long time today. It will be almost dark by the time we get to Nephtoah."

"You are right, but it was important, and we will make it. Where is Rangon?"

"Yonder." Mando pointed.

"Can you put the halters on the donkeys, while I speak a moment to the liveryman?"

"Sure. See: I remembered *not* to say, 'sir.'"

"Just remember to say it to everyone else who is older. Right?"

"Right."

Eskie sauntered to the liveryman's work bench. "Good afternoon. I am sorry Dagan could not come today. He really enjoyed working with the animals last time."

Rangon laid down his awl. "Is Dagan all right?"

Eskie met his eyes. "You noticed?"

"Yes. I saw him pressing his hand to his chest. What is wrong with him?"

"His father lambasted him with a fist to his chest." Anger boiled in Eskie's stomach.

"His ... father? Who is his father?"

"Ragar, the Amorite of Gibeon. ..."

Rangon's eyes widened, and his chin dropped.

"Do you know him? ... I have been thinking you sound like someone I know. Are you related to Ragar?"

"I am Ragar's brother. He stole my wife, when our son, Rango, was a young lad." Rangon gave a crooked smile. "That makes Rango and Dagan half brothers."

"I am sorry for your loss."

"Where is Ragar now?"

"He is at the Gibeonite wood camp at Mount Michmash. He is our main wood chopper."

"He was always a hot-tempered young man."

"He still is."

"Do you think Dagan can come again on market day?"

"I cannot say. He was growing worse, before we found out he was hurt. We are hoping he will get better with rest, so no more wood chopping for him. Will he be able to walk this far in two days? I cannot tell you."

Rangon entered his house and returned. "Take him this dried peppermint and make a tea for the pain. Tell him there is a place for him here anytime he is ready."

"Yes, sir. I will."

"Joshua ... [went on] to Hebron and attacked it. They took the city and put it to the sword." JOSHUA 10:36-37

Chapter 19
Essentials for Battle

Breaking camp at Rephaim ridge   *Sabbath Sunset, Day 13*

"Keshub."

"Yes, sir?"

"As soon as the rim of the sun reaches the horizon, Sabbath ends. We will break camp then. There will be a signaling whistle sent throughout the camp, when the sun is a hand's breadth above the horizon. That will be the cue to be ready. So let's enjoy the last of your fine lentil stew."

"Certainly." Keshub spread a small cloth on the ground and brought out the cold flat bread and mallow leaves he had saved. Uncovering the pottery bowl, he set it within reach of Joshua and folded his legs to sit on the ground across from him.

Joshua raised his face and hands toward heaven and prayed, with his eyes closed, *"Oh God. Bless this simple meal—a feast of your goodness to us. Bless the work you have led us to do. Thank you for your mercy and the Sabbath rest you provide. We beg your continued favor. Amen.*

"A second whistle will be time to break camp. You will take our gear to the camp of the Asherites in charge of wagons and supplies. March with them at the rear and help where you can. We will be trekking most of the night and will attack at dawn. When we reach our destination, the Asherite cooks will begin immediately to prepare to feed our soldiers. There will be plenty for you to do. Make yourself useful to the leader of the supply group." Joshua rose from their meal. "When I need you, I will send young Maki the Gadite.

"For now, until you hear the whistles, take a nap in the shade. I need to meet with Caleb and send out orders. If I am not here at sundown, proceed with your orders."

"Yes, sir."

Joshua zigzagged through the trees and disappeared among the men camping all around.

Keshub prayed, *God Most High, please protect master Joshua through the night's march and the battle. Thank you for his great faith in you. And please bless and protect Eskie, who is beginning to believe in you.*

Keshub checked for small rocks and acorns and unrolled his bedding. He stretched out, taking stock of their few items of comfort he would gather and stow with the transport wagons.

* * *

Keshub startled awake. In twilight, he packed their few things. He shrugged his own bedroll and knapsack on and slung the small bundle of camp items to his shoulder. The Asherites must be this way. He joined a stream of younger Hebrew soldiers, carrying camp gear. They flowed toward a circle of wagons confiscated from the towns they had conquered and filled with foodstuffs and gear. He hung back, knowing the others would likely check in their gear and hurry to rejoin their tribal camps.

Stepping forward, Keshub began, "Good evening, sir. I am

Keshub, Joshua's ..."

The Asherite in charge turned away, and another stepped in, half-turned away and giving orders over his shoulder to the man leaving.

... "Sir, I have orders to stay with your transport group ..."

"Keshub! We meet again." Mr. Amned, the Asherite leader on the pack train from Makkedah, grasped him by both shoulders for a double-cheek welcome.

"Yes, sir."

"So these are Joshua's things? I will stow them here in my wagon. See me when we make camp again. For now, help my men check all the cinches and the breast straps on the donkeys. I believe Mak is here somewhere, if you can find her. Our tribe being at the end, it will be a while before we move out, but be ready. We are marching at a fast pace tonight."

"Yes, sir."

"Whe-eet! Aram! Keshub, here. Give him a column next to you. He will inspect his own tack. He knows pack gear. All right?"

"Yes, sir!"

Keshub sensed the urgency in Amned.

"Keshub, right?" Aram gave him a scan, head to toe.

"Yes, sir."

"You are young to be on the march."

"Yes, sir. Joshua's Gibeonite servant. I travelled with Mr. Amned to join master Joshua."

"I see. You take this column of ten donkeys strung together."

"Yes, sir." Keshub took the lead rope of the first and checked her hobble. "Hello, Lady. Are you ready for an adventure tonight? ..."

... ... Marching at night with a thin sliver of crescent moon, Keshub delighted in the clip-clop rhythm of the donkeys. Joshua did not say where we are going. *God Most High, I take courage knowing Joshua is following you.*

෨෬

Dawn at Nephtoah Spring   *Day 15*

Eskie propped a knotty section of log, no good for bow making, on the rise behind Za'atar's rock house. Dew drops clinging to a spider's web among the reeds of the pond lit up with the sun's first rays. Tapping in an iron wedge first, he palmed the long, oaken handle of his host's basalt hammer and hoisted it over his shoulder. He smacked the iron with the basalt, and the log split without a splinter.

Leaning on the hammer handle, he picked up the piece and pitched it to a woodpile. He positioned another log and wedge for another blow.

"Could this not wait … until later."

"No, ma'am. I am sorry, but with Dagan hurt, I must. Reef and I are going hunting today, and I want to scout out the south ridge of the Rephaim Valley, too."

"Whack."

"So you will go to Jerusalem tomorrow?"

"Yes. It will be market day. Would you like me to take something for you or get something for you?"

"Whack."

"No, but I would like to go with you."

Eskie broke his swing and, turning, leaned on the handle. "Go with me?"

"Yes. I would like to visit my cousin for the day and come back with you when you return."

Eskie dipped his chin. "Certainly. If your father approves, I am at your service. If I get game today, we will need to start out as early as possible, to avoid the heat."

"Yes. I can do that. My cousin's brother will meet me at the spring and walk me to the craftsmen's valley."

"That is good. I may be with Jozman and Jebus all day."

"What do you do with them?"

He put the hammer in its place. "We are trying to devise a plan to avoid a battle with the Hebrews."

'Zalef turned both hands palm up. "Oh. Then help them some way."

Eskie placed his fists on his hips and bobbed his head. "It is that simple, is it?"

She shrugged, meeting his stare. "Maybe. ... Rosemary tea is ready." She turned and glided away around the house.

Could it be that simple?

* * *

Rephaim Ridge

Eskie scaled a limestone boulder the size of Za'atar's house, with a convenient leg up on Reef's hands. He flattened himself to the rock, as Reef joined him. "Is that Hebron there?"

"Yeah. Tallest mountain in Canaan."

"Have you ever been there?"

"Nah. The Rephaim and the Anakites do not mix."

"An old feud?"

"Something like that."

"Look. I see a faint trail beaten down in the grass, from below this ridge across the way. ... Straight to Hebron ... Is that smoke I see at Hebron?"

"Looks like it."

Eskie turned. "Would you like to go to Jerusalem with me tomorrow to deliver the fresh game?"

"Should I? What would I do?"

"You might meet a few widows. I am taking them so much meat to dry and smoke I am sure they need a lot of wood chopped."

Reef's giant smile transformed his gruesome features. "All

right. I will."

"Come to Nephtoah ... early morning?"

"I will be there."

"Today, I need to get our young buck home ..." Eskie dipped his chin. "Or back to Nephtoah."

Reef elbowed him in the ribs. "Unh-huh. I will help."

Eskie took one more look at Hebron. More smoke but not a conflagration. *The Hebrews are not burning the whole city. I wonder where Keshub is in all this.*

഼ᏆᏉ

At the battle for Hebron

Keshub shouldered an unfamiliar yoke, with two clay jars full of water—*clonkers*. Baba would have rejected these pots or would have put them back in the kiln to fire again on the next firing day. They did not have the Ra-eef' standard *clink*—evidence of a high-quality, high-fired vessel.

He tried not to listen to the battle in the distance on the slopes of Hebron. ... Memories flooded his mind. ... Five Gibeonites, with Baba in the lead, wearing ragged clothing and worn-out sandals. The Hebrews, a vast camp at Gilgal, and Joshua praying on a small rise nearby.

Baba had approached their leader, prepared to die if he must, but also in faith, knowing their god is not like men. Baba had held the secret Gran-baba had passed to him years before. A curse on the Hivites that we would become slaves. Baba had looked to the star whose name meant *the heretofore and the hereafter.* A god who remembers and who knows all.

Baba had asked for a treaty ... and had offered to serve. The curse of slavery became a gift—a gift of survival and a chance to know God Most High, creator of all good things.

"Mr. Amned, your water."

"Thank you, Keshub. Refill my jar in the wagon and my flask, and pour some in this crock to soak these dried palm fronds. I have pack gear with broken lashing that needs repair. The cooks will need more water, coming all day."

"Yes, sir."

"Carrying water, cooking, and making repairs are not exactly joining the fight, but the army cannot function without water, food, and pack gear. You are an essential part of God's army today, young man."

"Yes, sir." Keshub dispensed the water and headed back to the spring. *God Most High, protect Joshua. He fights your battle against evil and those who willfully oppose the knowledge of a holy and just creator God.*

*"Then Joshua and all Israel with him
turned around ..."* JOSHUA 10:38

Chapter 20
Taking Pickle Girl
to Jerusalem

Dawn at the lower spring of Hebron   *Day 15*

Keshub laid on more tinder and fanned the flame. Joshua and
his closest confidante talked in hushed tones nearby. After an all-
night march and yesterday's victory over Hebron, Joshua snored all
night. Keshub slept little, but, still, Joshua awoke early. He prayed
nearby, when Keshub first rolled over this morning.

Caleb nodded. "Good plan. Which will I take? The left or right?"
Joshua murmured.

Caleb unfolded his legs to stand and extended a hand to Joshua.

"Let's get started as soon as possible, friend." Joshua clasped
Caleb to him in a bear hug. "One more big push, before we can
take a short break to resupply. And God be with you."

"Yes, sir, and, with you too, friend. But remember: when all
this is done, I want ... *that* mountain." Caleb smiled and pointed
behind Joshua, where the battle for Hebron raged yesterday.

Joshua nodded. "You will have it. Moses promised."

Caleb turned and hurried away, with the vigor of a man half his eighty years.

Keshub extended a clay bowl. "Sir, do you have time for rosemary tea?"

"Only a gulp or two. You know what to do today. Report to Amned again. We are moving quickly again."

"Yes, sir." Keshub received the bowl and scurried to put out his fire and pack their gear. Another day of battle in Canaan. God Most High, protect master Joshua and your people.

80C8

Dawn at Nephtoah

Eskie held his Ra-eef' bowl of tea in both hands and tilted it. Two gulps and finished. He wiped his mouth and short beard with the back of his hand.

"Here is your vittles bag for later." 'Zalef's soft voice still surprised him, since her first words when they met challenged him with, "Who are you?" and, "Why are you lurking about?"

"I will be with Jozman. I am sure he will offer some hospitality and refreshment. I could give this to Mando and Dagan."

She dropped her eyelids and long lashes to her cheeks. "They have theirs. Yours has two pickled ducks' eggs to share with what Uncle Jozman has to offer."

"Oh. I do like your pickled eggs. What if I do not want to share?"

"Then you will be a selfish pig." Her eyes opened wide. "It will be your decision. I will get my knapsack, and I am ready."

Eskie grinned as she returned to the house. He tucked the vittles into his bag and checked the donkeys' gear and tie-downs. "Mando, are you ready?"

"Yes, s-s-s. Brother. I cannot seem to change old habits." Mando waggled his head.

"Am I going too?" Dagan bit the side of his lower lip.

"How do you feel?"

"Some better." He rubbed the right side of his chest. "Still a twinge when I turned over and got out of my bedroll."

"Can you walk from here to Jerusalem without making your injury worse again? We cannot leave you beside the trail halfway there. And I must meet with Jozman today."

"Hallow!" Reef approached from behind.

Eskie turned. The giant wore that smile again. *I hope his expectations are not too high.* "Good morning. Let me check with Za'atar for a moment. I think we are ready." Eskie strode to the woodchopping hillock. "Sir, do you have a walking stick or a crutch I can borrow for Dagan?"

Za'atar leaned his hammer on a log and sauntered to a row of pegs wedged in crevices between the rocks of his house. "Will this do?"

Eskie grabbed the oaken walking stick and stepped a few steps to gauge how much help it would be for Dagan. "If it only keeps him steady on his feet, it will be a help."

"Mind you, take good care of my daughter today."

Eskie startled and looked his host in the eye. "Yes, sir. You can be sure I will."

Za'atar grasped him by his shoulders and connected to either cheek. "She is precious to me." His words, soft and few, conveyed deep meaning.

Eskie met his eyes straight on. "And to me, also, sir."

'Zalef's father nodded, without a smile, and stepped back.

"Sir, I wish you would go with us. I would like for you to be included in the discussion of Jerusalem's defense today."

Za'atar lowered his chin and squinted. "Lad, what I do best is turn mighty trees to strong bow-making material. Having more quality bows than the front line of the advancing enemy is my contribution to the defense of Jerusalem."

"Yes, sir." Eskie pivoted and escaped to the front of the house, where all assembled. He tossed Za'atar's walking stick. "Let us know if you start to feel worse."

Dagan's smile broke out of a worried face. He grinned from ear to ear.

"Dagan, you set the pace. We want to be there by or before midday, but we also have a gentlewoman with us. Mando and Reef, bring up the rear with the donkeys. Is that good for you?"

"Like a stroll before breakfast." Reef smiled that gap-toothed smile again.

Eskie extended his elbow to steady 'Zalef on the rocky path. Her touch sent fire racing through his being.

"Eskie, tell me about your family. Do you have brothers and sisters? You have stayed at my home for several days, and I know nothing about you. You could be a wandering ruffian, for all I know."

"You would think that even after I came to your rescue on the day we met?"

"I was not in danger."

"I did not know that. You *sounded* like you were in mortal danger. That was a bloodcurdling scream you let out. I never before heard such a scream."

She tossed her head and glanced up at him. "Do you always exaggerate this way?"

"Umm. Maybe. My mother may have said before if my mouth is open, I am exaggerating."

"I thought so. Tell me about your mother." … …

* * *

"Eskie! Good hunting again?" Jozman clapped him on the shoulder and greeted him with the traditional cheek-to-cheek gesture.

"Yes, sir. And this is my friend Reef. He knows all the best trails and wallows in the forest of Rephaim. I could not have this continued success without him."

With creases appearing beside his mouth, Jozman gazed up at the giant woodsman. "So you are the fellow who wants a wife—or five?"

Reef gulped. "Yez, sir."

"No one has volunteered yet, but I hear some are discussing your offer."

Eskie nudged Reef's meaty elbow. "We thought maybe Reef could chop some wood for your cooking fires today." He stifled a smile but arched his eyebrows high. "Maybe a little getting acquainted at a distance could help move things along a bit."

Jozman stepped to the doorway. "Yaakoub, take this young man out back to the woodpile and find him our best axe and a helper."

"Yes, sir." Yaakoub's eyes widened, and his chin rose when he saw Reef. "Yes, sir!"

Jozman turned back and eased into his cushioned place at the reed floor covering. He twisted a smile. "As much wood chopping and smoking and drying of meat as we are doing, anyone would think we are expecting a long siege."

Eskie folded into place across from him. "I am hoping there will be no need for a siege. Is Jebus joining us today?"

"He should be here soon. While we wait, tell me about your little brother being part of the Hebrew camp. And about the Gibeonite alliance with the Hebrews." Jozman leaned back, with arms crossed.

Eskie nodded. "Sir, my little brother, Keshub, was part of the delegation my father put together to approach the Hebrews at Gilgal. At a short distance away, he held the lead ropes of our donkeys carrying gifts, while our men spoke with Joshua."

"What about the old sandals and old clothing we heard about?"

"The worn-out clothing was part of the ruse of having come

from a far distance. I heard Moses—on the day he died on Mount Nebo—say their god told them to destroy all the nations of this land."

"You heard that?"

"Yes, Jebus and I watched together from the top of Nebo that day. We scrambled to flee, when we realized Moses and Joshua were coming there. But I hid to see them up close and heard the plan from Moses's lips."

Jozman arched his brows high. "The Hebrews appear to be following the plan."

"Yes, sir, they are."

"So why is your brother in their camp?"

"Sir, three days later, they found out we lived only a day's march away. Three more days, and they brought their whole army to attack us." His voice broke. He swallowed hard.

"Our whole valley moved to Gibeon's summit for a doomed defense against their attack. My father and the delegation, including my little brother, made camp near the ridgeline, where Joshua would first see our small, unwalled city below. Baba waited, unarmed, calmly making sandals for our family.

"When Joshua demanded an explanation, Baba said we had seen how powerful his god is and how he fights the Hebrews' battles for them. He offered our service. Joshua pronounced all of Gibeon to be woodcutters and water carriers for their house of god. Baba agreed."

"Your father is an amazing man. A rare mix of courage and humility."

Eskie bowed his head. "Baba did not count on Joshua's next move. He demanded Keshub as his personal slave—to satisfy the elders of his people. Joshua took him as a hostage to be sure Baba kept his word. After that, we set up the wood camp in the forest of Mount Michmash and began daily deliveries of donkey trainloads of wood to Gilgal. That is how I learned of their practice of a

Sabbath day of rest."

"So when the Amorite kings came to attack Gibeon?"

"Baba sent me to claim the benefit of our treaty with the Hebrews. I found Joshua praying, and he acted like he was expecting me. He said his god had already told him to go to Gibeon. He said God promised him a great victory."

"Eskie, you tell an interesting tale, but my question in all this is where does your loyalty lie? Are you for us or against us?"

Eskie met Jozman's gaze. "Sir, I counted it a great adventure to help my friend Jebus return to Jerusalem and free his father from the king's dungeon. In the time I have stayed in Za'atar's household and have tasted 'Zalef's cooking, this has become much more to me than an adventure.

"You are questioning my encounter with my brother in the forest of Rephaim. It was mere happenstance. That is unless the one who directs the white owl who sits in the pine tree by the dung gate directed me there. Keshub told me nothing. I told him I was hunting to help feed the widows and orphans living in the Amorite king's palace since the Jebusites took over. And I told him you hanged the murdering men of Molech on Molech's own contraption."

Eskie grinned. "Baba thinks highly of the integrity and character of Joshua. Letting Joshua know of the integrity and character of the Jebusites has to be a stone for us on the scales of justice."

Jozman gave a slow nod.

"Have you heard from Hebron? I think we were right about the Hebrews' going there yesterday. I saw several large fires at Hebron from the forest ridge, though certainly nothing like Jericho. And I have an idea." … … …

"They took [Debir], its king and its villages, and put them to the sword. Everyone in it they totally destroyed." JOSHUA 10:39

Chapter 21
Jebusite Council

Near Jerusalem   *Day 15*

Eskie descended into Kidron Valley with a hand on the shoulder of Mando. "How did Dagan fare today, brother?"

"Good, I think. Mr. Rangon cautioned him often to go slowly and not to overdo. He also ordered Dagan to play goat's knuckles in the shade with his son a good bit of time, especially during the hottest time of day. Where is Reef?"

"He is still at the palace. He will meet us at the livery. He chopped wood for the kitchen fires, and whoa! That man can truly split wood like lightning. I think he impressed the widows. I know he impressed their children. Quite a number gathered around to watch, with eyes wide. Here we are."

Eskie rapped on the rough-hewn door with the impressive peephole. "Naqib. Eskie from Gibeon here."

The door swung back, and 'Zalef stood in the sunshine, dark eyes full of mirth. Her cousins peeked around a door frame and waved good-byes.

Eskie pulled the door closed behind them, while girlish giggles erupted inside the courtyard. "Where is your uncle?"

"He had business a few houses away, and here he comes now."

"Eskie, thank you for escorting my niece for a visit today. Here is my son. He will accompany you across Mount Moriah. He has a basket of cucumbers and melons for Za'atar's supper."

"Thank you, sir. I am glad to help." Eskie drew Naqib aside. "Can we talk a moment, sir? Privately?

"Jozman received a runner, as I was leaving today. Joshua's army attacked Hebron yesterday, as we expected. They defeated the best stronghold of Canaan, which was not what we had hoped for. Today the Hebrews have turned around in two columns, to march to Debir.

"At last sighting, Hebron's detachment of perhaps Canaan's best soldiers was heading back to Hebron. That sounds like Joshua's two battle groups have set an ambush to surround and annihilate what is left of Hebron. Jozman wants a council first thing tomorrow morning. He would like you to be there."

Naqib combed his fingers through his shock of graying hair. "I understand. Will I see you there?"

"Yes, sir, you will. If I can talk him into it, I hope Za'atar's household will move inside the walls of Jerusalem soon. Perhaps your families here, also."

"We will see. It is not far for us. Nephtoah is not so close."

* * *

"Eskie, you look so serious. What is happening?" 'Zalef's dark eyes penetrated his heart.

He tucked her hand into the crook of his elbow. For a moment, he allowed his hand to remain on hers. "These are serious times— no exaggeration. The Hebrew army has completely conquered Jericho, Ai, Makkedah, Libnah, Lachish, Eglon, and Hebron and has left no survivors in any of those cities. Tomorrow we believe they will attack Debir."

At the threshing floor at the pinnacle of Mount Moriah, Eskie raised his eyes to the sun making its regular descent toward the Great Sea. "After that, most likely Jerusalem."

"They are the same army who rescued Gibeon? Why Gibeon?"

"Because my father asked for a treaty."

"So … they are approachable."

* * *

Nephtoah at dawn   *Day 16*

Whack. Eskie bent and tossed a split log to the woodpile.

Whack. …

Whack. …

Whack. …

"Why are you doing that? There is no need. We have no game to smoke today. And we are all going to Jerusalem, right?"

Eskie lifted his eyes and sucked in a deep breath. Her soft voice stirred emotions new to him. Delight. … Worry. … Fear. "I could not sleep. I decided to stretch my muscles, before I am obliged to sit in a meeting all day."

"Your tea is ready. Please come."

* * *

Eskie followed behind Za'atar, who led his donkey laden with staves ready to be formed into bows. Mando brought up the rear with the Ra-eef' donkey. Eskie held, in one hand, a lead rope for a donkey burdened with all the foodstuffs 'Zalef could pull together overnight. On his other side, 'Zalef clasped his elbow. "Thank you for agreeing to return to the craftsmen's valley. I am glad Dagan stayed with Rangon yesterday. Mando and I will probably stay there tonight. Or wherever we can spread a bedroll."

"Are you certain you are not exaggerating the threat?" Her soft tone voiced the question without accusation.

"We will surely receive a report today of the Hebrews at Debir. The attackers at Gibeon included Lachish, Debir, Eglon, Hebron, and Jerusalem, all walled cities whose kings attacked our city at dawn that day. I doubt the Hebrews will count their mission done, until they confront Jerusalem, too."

"So the main Hebrew camp is at Gilgal, on the Jordan River. How many days has their army been away from home?"

"Sixteen. If they stay true to their previous pattern, they will begin a march to Jerusalem tomorrow morning. You and your cousins may be spending tomorrow night inside the walls of Jerusalem."

"I will count this a rare treat to spend more time with my cousins today, even if we are preparing for a siege. Tomorrow will take care of itself when it comes."

"That sounds very near to what my father has said. At the risk of sounding like my father, 'We will prepare for what we can prepare for and endure with integrity what we cannot prepare for.'"

"I can see you are your father's son. Remember, your father found a way. You will, too."

* * *

Eskie led Za'atar to Jozman's council room. Eskie lowered himself to a place beside Jebus.

Jozman cleared his throat. "Men, this is a day of great uncertainty."

Naqib spoke first. "What is our last report of the Hebrews?"

"A runner came before the dew dried this morning. He confirmed the Hebrews ambushed Hebron's first division yesterday, at midday, as they returned from Debir. The Hebrews left no survivors. By nightfall, they had surrounded Debir. At first light today, they attacked."

"So there will be a report of the destruction of Debir tonight?" Naqib stared at the mat.

With one foot flat on the mat and one knee up, Jozman leaned an elbow on it. "I refuse to give up before the Hebrews get here. What can we do?"

Za'atar quipped, "Hand-to-hand combat is not a solution."

Naqib still examined the mat. "We have a wall, but so did Hebron, Lachish, Ai ... and Jericho ... "

Eskie cleared his throat and waited to be recognized. With no Jebusite blood to spill and being the youngest in the room, he must choose his words with care. *Sir, I could use some help here. Please.*

Jozman levelled his forearm on his knee. "Gentlemen, our young Gibeonite friend and I have talked at length about his observations of the Hebrews. His father led the delegation that sought a treaty with them at Gilgal. He has met their leader, Joshua, and I have questioned him closely to determine where his loyalties lie. I trust him, and I believe he may have insights for our situation. Eskie, tell them what you told me about the Hebrew army's weapons."

"Yes, sir. I watched the Hebrews circle Jericho every day for seven days. Mostly, they carried clubs, and farm tools—except for the first unit, which always leads into battle."

Za'atar narrowed his eyes. "What was different about the lead unit?"

Eskie leaned forward. "They carried weapons made for war and appeared to know how to use them."

Jozman stared at the mat. "The Hebrews have won every battle. They leave no survivors, and they add to their arsenal of weapons."

"Except for the battle at Ai, sir. Remember? I saw the Hebrews turn and run—after losing about thirty men. They straggled back to Gilgal, discouraged and defeated. That is when my father reasoned they are but men, like we are."

Jebus pointed. "Uncle Zee, this is where yours and Baba's new project will be exactly what we need when we meet the Hebrews— face-to-face."

Za'atar's eyes widened. "You are right! Perfect."

Eskie's head swiveled from one to the other. "Tell us. What is it?"

"A longer bow, that, with strong bowmen, can shoot an arrow much farther than any bow we have made before." Jebus spoke with confidence. "Perhaps as far as from the wall to an enemy across the Kidron Valley."

"How many bows like this do we have?" Jozman leaned forward.

"Ten. We have kept them hidden, though." Za'atar looked to Jebus for confirmation.

"Do you have ten archers who can use them?" The hairs on Eskie's arms rose.

Jebus nodded. "We do. We practice every third day in the olive grove, near Uncle 'Raunah's threshing floor."

"Sir, I quote my friend and mentor, Sir Ghaleb. He says, 'When your defense is dismal' … and ours is, when we look at the difference in numbers. 'You must develop an offense that will maximize your strengths and minimize your weaknesses.' So what if …?"

Looking down still, Naqib interrupted, "There is something else we must do first … " Then he hesitated.

Za'atar slapped the mat twice and got Naqib's attention. "Brother, I know you. You are rolling an idea over in the depth of your bowels. Spit it out."

Naqib raised his eyes to the wattle ceiling. "Our wall is too low. We need a higher wall all around, but that we cannot do in time if we are attacked in two days. We need a more immediate fix at the main gate … with a tower. So we can actually see the bottom of the Kidron Valley and the Ben Hinnom Valley. We must not lose sight of the enemy, as they come up the steep ravine to attack."

Jozman rubbed his forehead. "Zedek ordered me to stockpile stones to raise the wall, but we do not have enough to start. Perhaps we have enough stones to build a tower, though. Can we have it ready in two days?"

Naqib levelled his gaze at Jozman. "We can turn out all our men to move the stones and timbers into place, and all our stonemasons can begin immediately."

Jozman took charge. "Naqib and Jebus, get word to all the men in the craftsmen's valley. Za'atar and Eskie, come with me to the main gate. We will all meet again at the storage cave near Gihon Spring."

Eskie scrambled to his feet and followed Jozman and Za'atar. *Sir, there is surely no moment to spare to build a tower so quickly. Help us all.*

"They left no survivors. They did to Debir and its king as they had to Libnah and its king and to Hebron." JOSHUA 10:39

Chapter 22
Building the Jebusite Tower

Early morning near Debir   *Day 17*

Keshub sniffed the dewy air, while he waited in line at the Asherite cook tents. Umm. Garlicky bean paste—with hot flat bread. *Smells like home.*

"Hey, sprout. What are you doing in this mighty army? Why are you not back at Gilgal with your ma-ma?"

"Stick a cork in it, Dan-ite. That is Joshua's personal aide." The cook grimaced at Keshub and slapped a wooden paddle full on the Danite's extended vessel. "Move along, man. *That is* your portion today."

"For you, young man, … Keshub, right?"

"Yes, sir."

"And for commander Joshua … a double portion."

"Thank you. May God Most High shower you with blessings."

"Oh, he has! He has. Five sons back at Gilgal."

Keshub wrapped their food in a cloth to keep it warm. He zig-zagged through the camp to the small fire near his and Joshua's bedrolls. Eskie raked a flat rock from the edge of the fire and placed the cloth-bound food on the heated stone.

He sighted Joshua yonder, on a small rise. Praying. He poured a bowl of hot rosemary tea and trod with care, not to slosh any out. "Sir?"

… "Keshub?"

"Your tea, sir?"

Joshua rubbed his eyes with thumb and forefinger at the bridge of his nose. "Yes … thank you."

Keshub delivered the tea and stepped back. "Thank you, sir."

Joshua slurped … and lifted his eyes above the rim of the bowl—surprised. "You are thanking me?"

"Yes, sir. It is a privilege to serve a man who talks to God Most High, like you do."

"Pray he continues to talk to me, Keshub."

"I do, sir."

෨෬

Jerusalem

Eskie opened his eyes to streaks of pink. The color brought to mind Gran-mamaa's roses beside the Ra-eef' guest house back in Gibeon. Rangon's banty rooster voiced his interpretation of a half-strangled creature in the liveryman's livestock pen. Eskie breathed deeply of the smell of good, clean garbage burning in the Hinnom nearby. "Mmm. Is that also pork back fat I smell? Mando?"

Mando's bedroll near him on Rangon's roof lay open, but vacant. Eskie drew up his knees to his chest and rocked to a seated position. He tied on his sandals, crossed his ankles, and stood to roll up his blankets and stow them away.

Descending Rangon's rickety ladder, he spied Mando hanging over the sizzle on Rangon's flat stone at the cook fire. "Boy-dough, go up top and stow your blankets away from the overhanging tree branches, lest birds roost there today." He raised his eyebrows high.

Mando's expression evolved to understanding. He scurried to take care of his things.

Eskie approached the cooking fire. "Good morning, Rangon. How are you this morning?"

The cook at the fire turned to him, scowling.

Eskie startled. "Rango? So you are the cook."

"Baba and Dagan are watering the livestock. I offered to turn the pork belly. There is so little I can do with this useless leg of mine."

"It must be difficult, man."

"It is, and even though the pain is great, I hear myself complain way too much. Having Mando and Dagan here and playing goats' knuckles with them, I have realized it hurts less if I do something, anything, to get my mind off the pain and what I have lost."

"Man, that is excellent. There are bound to be other things you will find to do, too."

"Ez-gee!"

"Reef! Wha-a?" Eskie stopped, no words would come out. The big man pulled two sapling poles as big around as Eskie's calf. Surely, no two men from Jerusalem could pull the weight of the fresh game he had strapped to his conveyance. "Whoa, man. You will surely get a wife soon with all this!"

The boyish, gap-toothed grin spread across his rugged face.

"You must have started toward Jerusalem at the crack of dawn to be here so early."

"I camped at Nephtoah last night."

Eskie eyed Reef's gear. "Is there any way … I can help? I can go with you to the palace."

"Good. I would rather you do the talking part."

"Sure, man. I have never been accused of having nothing to say—although, many times, I should have kept my mouth shut."

* * *

Eskie corralled his mirth as they neared Jerusalem's main gate, where heavy stones lay stacked all about. Already several Jebusite men laid stones next to the city wall. He gave a sidewise glance Reef's way. *That man has awesome strength. I wonder ....*

Jozman raised his eyes when he heard them approaching with saplings scraping along the stone-paved road to Gihon Spring. "Reef! More fresh game? We may have to make you king for a day around here. I hope when you get a wife—and you surely will— you will continue to hunt for us sometimes, if we are still here." Jozman gave a shrug.

Reef grinned.

"Sir, I will take Reef to the palace and will be back soon." Inside the gate. "Did you hear that, Reef? They may make you king for a day here." Eskie reached high and slapped the gentle giant on his back.

"What were all the stones for?"

"We are building a tower near the main gate. Yesterday, the Hebrews defeated Debir. They may be coming back this way today. If so, they could attack here as soon as tomorrow."

"Tomorrow?"

"Maybe. We will know more when we get word of what they are doing today." Eskie shook his head. "There are so many of them— multitudes. We are just trying to survive. My father found a way in Gibeon when no one believed we could. I am asking the Hebrew god to make a way for us here, too."

"You believe in their god?"

"Reef, you remember ten plus seven days ago?"

"No, what?"

"The day that lasted nearly two days?"

"Oh, yes. We crept into our caves—sure the sun was about to fall to earth. What do you know about that?"

"That was the day Zedek and the Amorites attacked Gibeon, and the Hebrews kept their word and defended us in Aijalon Valley."

"I heard about that. That was the same day the sun stayed still over us?"

Eskie nodded. "Joshua prayed to their god and asked him to stop the sun from going down. He wanted to capture the Amorites, who were fleeing over Beth Horon Pass. The sun stayed in place, and the Hebrews executed all five kings the next day."

"Whoa. Who could fight that kind of army?"

"Exactly." … … …

Eskie slapped Reef on the back again. "Hey, man. I saw eyes light up in the kitchen when you entered. You may go home with a family today."

"Ez-gee, do not tease me. This is serious."

"I know, man. I do not mean to tease. I need to see Jozman. Will you chop wood?"

"Nah. I will help with the tower."

* * *

Eskie quickened his steps to rejoin Reef and laughed aloud, as he caught sight of him working with two stone workers. He stood head and shoulders taller than those big men. Together, using Reef's saplings, they made quick work of moving stones to the growing tower.

Sir, if only Reef and his new wives survive an attack tomorrow, it will have been a fight worth fighting. But, sir, I ask you to consider these good people.

Eskie emptied the contents of his leather knapsack. He loaded it with smaller spacer stones used to fill in gaps to level each course of bigger stones. He stood by one of the expert stonemasons, trying to guess the size of the rock he needed next. He glanced at his shadow, as a runner appeared from the Kidron in late afternoon.

"Eskie!"

He stepped aside, to give his place to another carrier of spacer rocks, and looked for Jozman, who had called his name. He assessed their progress so far. "Sir, using the existing wall instead of a stand-alone tower is yielding many advantages. Maybe there is a chance for us."

With arms crossed on his chest, Jozman directed Eskie with a nod to hear the young man beside him.

The sweat-soaked relayer eyed Eskie and stretched taller. He appeared to be about Eskie's age. "Sirs, we expected to receive one of four messages from our observer near Debir. If he runs toward the rising sun ..."

Eskie interrupted. "Joshua's army is going toward the Salt Sea."

The runner nodded. "If he runs toward the setting sun ..."

"They are going toward the Great Sea."

"If he runs down the hill toward us a little way ..."

"Hebrews—coming our way." Eskie nodded, hands at his hips.

"Or if the eye witness disappears over the hill away from us for a moment."

"That means they are going farther away. Which one was it?" Eskie gestured with an open palm.

"None of those."

"What? The Hebrews have not moved all day?" Eskie scratched his head.

"Yes, sir." The runner met Eskie's gaze for the first time. "After the yodeler said, 'Hall-oo! ' three times, he sat down, then lay down. He repeated the same signal three times."

"What do you think it means that the Hebrews have not started this way yet?" Jozman raised his fist to his mouth.

Eskie counted on his fingers, then took out a short rope from his sling-stone bag at his waist. "It is too soon for them to stay in place for the Sabbath." He checked the knots again. "Sabbath will be the third day from now. If they come this way at first light tomorrow, they could attack the next day, but that day is their preparation day for Sabbath. They must cook enough on preparation day to have enough to feed the army for two days. I ... doubt they would attack on preparation day, but, of course, I could be wrong,"

"So we can be sure they cannot attack on the morrow, because they are still camped at Debir." Jozman leaned his head back. "That is excellent news."

"Yes, sir. And we should know by midday tomorrow, if they are coming here."

Loud whistles sounded from the area of the main gate.

Jozman dropped his arms and clapped the runner's shoulder. "Wait a moment, lad, and have dinner with our men, before you return to your lookout station. Roasted venison and ibex tonight."

"Yes, sir!"

Eskie returned to the building site, where the kitchen steward got everybody's attention with another piercing whistle.

"Gentlemen, would two of you escort Reef from Rephaim Valley here for me?"

Reef looked from side to side, as the nearest two stonemasons led him by the arm to the lower course of the tower.

"Come up here, sir, and take a seat of honor on top of the wall of Jerusalem."

Murmurs ran through the herd of sweaty workers at the base.

Reef hesitated. Unsure.

"Re-eef, Re-eef, Re-eef ... ..."

At the top of the wall, the steward bowed and directed Reef to sit, then placed a laurel wreath on his head. "Reef of Rephaim Forest, we crown you king of Jerusalem till sundown. Thank you for your assistance in building the tower today. And we thank you for your very great kindness toward the needs of our widows and orphans for the last several days. You have saved us from famine, to be sure."

"Hear, hear!" The tower crew affirmed the steward's announcement.

He put up his hand for quiet. "One more thing, friend."

Reef levelled his gaze to the steward ... who waited a moment, then directed Reef's eyes to look over his right shoulder and see something inside the city wall.

The giant's mouth dropped, and his eyes popped wide. The gap-toothed grin appeared wider than ever.

"Reef, please go inside the city gate and meet your great reward for your very kind heart."

Reef descended the several stair-stepped courses of stones and looked around. "Ez-gee?"

"Here, man." Eskie stepped to his friend's side.

"Will you go in with me? I might not know what to say."

"So, Joshua [marched into the Negev and] *subdued the whole region, ... just as the Lord ... commanded."* JOSHUA 10:40

Chapter 23
The Gift of More Time

Jerusalem   *Day 18*

Eskie rubbed the sleepiness out of his eyes and chuckled. The strangled-sounding rooster woke him, but the memory of Reef leaving Jerusalem yesterday *with a family* made him laugh.

Reef's extra-strong sapling conveyance held all the gear the five women owned. Two knee-high sprouts straddled each shoulder and held on to his beard and hair for dear life. His grin—unstoppable. The big man had a family of his own at last.

Eskie surprised himself with his own moistened eyes and rubbed the melancholy evidence away with the heels of his hands. He rolled out of his bedroll and started his day. ... ...

Eskie gulped from a bowl of tea offered by the liveryman's son. "Man, that is the best tea ever. What is in it?"

Rango smiled a rare smile, for him. "Just dried peppermint leaves and a bit of honey from the bees in that Cassia tree yonder."

"Well, you could have a booth at market day to sell this. People would line up."

Eskie angled across the livestock pen to where Dagan raked up dung for the pile nearby. "Dagan, how are you feeling?"

"Better, I think. I am leading the animals to the wadi to drink instead of carrying heavy water jars. And I am not chopping wood yet. Rangon makes me rest, so I know you told him."

"Yes, I did. I am glad you are better. Take care." He strolled to where Rangon brushed a fine animal. "Morning. How is Dagan working out for you here?"

Rangon hesitated a moment and returned to brushing. "Dagan loves the animals and is good with them. He gets along well with Rango, too."

"Have you told them they are brothers?"

"No. I am a coward. Would it be better or worse if they knew they are brothers? My brother and I fought like wild cats."

"I do not know about that, but are you committed to including him in your family? Dagan never had any place where he felt he belonged. Besides him being related, it seems to me you and Rango need him, if he will stay."

Rangon bit his lip and said nothing.

* * *

Eskie sauntered up to the tower in progress at the main gate to Jerusalem. He rolled his shoulders and stretched his elbows to the front and back. He fell into step with the stonemason he worked with yesterday. "Morning. Do you think we can finish today?"

"That depends on whether Jozman decides it is tall enough and how close an attack may be."   ...   ...

"Eskie!"

He turned from filling his knapsack again with spacer stones and checked his shadow for time. Noon. Jozman motioned him to come. *Please, sir. Help us.*

This runner resembled the one yesterday—but a little older,

perhaps. *Maybe they are family.* Eskie detected the sweaty new arrival's squint toward him—questioning his value in the discussion of the message.

Jozman tilted his head toward Eskie. "Tell Eskie what you told me."

"The yodeler hallooed three times and ran away on the backside of his hill. Moments later, he returned and repeated the same message."

Jozman placed his hands at his hips. "So how long do you think we have now?"

Eskie drew a deep breath and blew it out with puffed-out cheeks. "First question, where are they going? Not to Egypt, surely. Or the Sinai. But what towns are in the direction of Egypt?"

Jozman rubbed his chin. "There is Arad, although the Hebrews defeated them about this time last year. I cannot imagine they will put up much of a battle one year later."

"What else?"

"The largest are Hormah and Beersheba. They and Arad are somewhat isolated by the terrain. Together, the three are in a valley of good land for growing wheat."

Eskie nodded. "That might be reason enough to go there. The Hebrews must feed their families, just like we do. And the multitude still in camp back at Gilgal could be running short on supplies. Also, this plays to our favor, since Sir Ghaleb says an army guarding a large amount of supplies cannot travel as quickly as battalions of foot soldiers."

* * *

Eskie tucked his hands near his armpits, trying not to fidget. He stared at the pattern of woven reeds they all sat on. His idea, interlaced with Jebusite skills and resources, still sounded good. At least his proposed plan sounded good to him. He searched again for a fatal flaw, as Jozman presented the daring confrontation to the others.

"And who will go out to meet Joshua's army on the other side of en-Rogel?" Naqib, always the practical one, voiced the question for all of them.

Jozman cleared his throat and glanced Eskie's way. "I will. Who will go with me?"

Jebus already knew the plan. "I will demonstrate the range of the longbow for their consideration."

"I will. Joshua made a treaty with my father at Gilgal. I will remind him of that, as we seek his favor and his god's mercy."

Jozman surveyed the group. "Is there any other advantage we can employ? … Anything?"

Eskie laid out his rope with knots. He hiked up one knee and leaned his chin on it, with his hands clasped at his ankle. "They left their families in their camp at Gilgal ten plus eight days ago. … They will be travelling more slowly, as they head back to Gilgal. Why? … Jozman says the cities of the Negev are rich with a fresh harvest of wheat at this time of year. The Hebrew army will be moving many wagons and donkey trains laden with loot and grain.

"Have you ever walked beside your donkey, as you returned to your home … and his? The closer you got to home, the donkey pulled harder on the lead rope. The animal knew the end of the journey was near. Shedding his burden, fresh water, and comfort were ahead. … I believe the Hebrew soldiers will feel the same, when they know they are only one day's walk from home camp at Gilgal."

Jebus gave Eskie's knee a nudge with his fist. "So you think battle-hardened soldiers will pass us by because they are homesick?"

Eskie righted himself, with the loss of his knee as prop, and grinned. "Maybe. As my baba says, 'They are but men … like us. First, we demonstrate we will hold our ground and fight until our last man is standing. Second, we show them our best defensive strategy—the longbows on the tower. This alone will surely cause a significant loss to their lead units. Then we convince them of our ability to do what we threaten to do, when you show your expert marksmanship. If they stand down, and we pray they will, we treat them with hospitality that says, 'We will be your neighbors.'

"We will make them think even more about home and family. We give them home goods for gifts to their loved ones. What do we have to lose? A battle with them for possession of Jerusalem—us against them—would never end up in our favor."

...

Jozman grinned and nodded. "What do we have, men, that will cause these fierce soldiers to bring their softer emotions to the surface?"

Naqib: "Small bows and arrows for their sons."

Za'atar: "Pickled duck's eggs for their fathers or mothers."

Jebus: "Hair ribbons for their wives and daughters."

Eskie chuckled, "Olive oil soap—for cleaning up for their sweethearts."

The others looked at each other and nodded, grinning. Naqib spoke for them all. "A wagon full of olive oil soap.

"And whatever else our people can give for the peace of Jerusalem. Let's adjourn for dinner, men."

...

"Sir?" Eskie faced Jozman, as the others filed out of the room.

Jozman turned and draped an arm across his back. "Son. I think this might actually work."

"Sir, I hope so. But I have a request." Eskie sucked in a deep breath.

Jozman lowered his chin. "Go ahead."

"Sir, I would like to go home to Gibeon to see my family again. Perhaps I can bring back some of the Amorite armies' weapons left on the battlefield in Aijalon Valley. And ... I need to seek my father's wisdom in all this."

"Of course. Will you go alone?"

"I will take Mando with me. He needs to meet his new family there."

Jozman looked away, and his prominent throat lump moved up, then down. "Are you sure you want to return here?"

"Sir, I will return in three days. I will be back before the Hebrews arrive."

"Son, I would not blame you if you did not return. This plan for Jebusite survival is no sure thing."

෨෬

Debir, near sunset

"Keshub, did commander Joshua give you orders?" Mr. Amned stirred the coals of the evening fire.

"Yes, sir. He told me to help you in any way you can use me on the trek to Hebron tomorrow and until Mr. Phinehas arrives. If the son of the high priest is in Hebron, or when he arrives, I am to serve him like I serve master Joshua."

"I see. We will leave before dawn tomorrow, so we can arrive near Hebron before the Sabbath begins at sundown. Have your assigned donkeys ready."

"Yes, sir. I will."

෨෬

Livery stable of Jerusalem at sunset

"Did you hear the news, Eskie?" A smile lurked at the corners of Dagan's mouth.

Eskie wanted to hear it from Dagan himself. "What news? The Hebrews went deeper in the Negev today, and the threat of annihilation is not immediate—for a while?"

"No."

194

"The Jebusite tower is completed and work starts tomorrow on raising the height of the wall all around?"

"No. Not that news, either." Dagan actually grinned.

"Then what? What could possibly be news at the livery stable? Did the banty rooster lay an egg today?"

"No-o. … I have a brother."

"You have a brother. I have five of those, counting Mando." Eskie winked. "How did you find that out?"

"Rangon told me today. And he said I have a home here as long as I want. Did you know already?"

"Yes, he told me a few days ago. Does Rango know, too?"

Dagan smiled, nodding. "Yes. Rangon told us both at the same time. We looked at each other, and … somehow, we were not surprised. Now I feel a connection to my mother I have never had before. Does that make any sense?"

Eskie realized for the first time Dagan and he were eye to eye. "I guess that means you are not interested in going to Gibeon with me."

"Uncle Rangon and Rango need me here." His voice cracked, and he looked away. He twitched his nose and looked back. "I have never truly been needed anywhere before. I have to stay."

"So Joshua [went to] *subdue the whole region* [of the Negev near Arad. And Joshua prepared for the Sabbath.]" JOSHUA 10:40

Chapter 24
There Is No Place Like Home

On the trail to Gibeon   *Day 19*

"Eskie?" Mando led two donkeys clip-clopping on the limestone trail.

Eskie glanced back over his shoulder. "Hunh?"

"What will your baba and mamaa think about you adopting me into the family? Will they be angry?"

"Angry? Of course not. They like scrawny little mutts like you. You just eat what is put in front of you. Tell my mother it is the best you have ever tasted in your whole life—which it will be, I guarantee. They will love you, man, but remember: no talking, while we eat. That is a rule. Besides, if you talk, you will miss your turn to dip your flat bread in the bowl. I know. I learned the hard way."

"Tell me again all their names."

"Well, there is Mattah, about your age, and his older brother, Lehab. They are our cousins—Uncle Samir's boys. Uncle Samir is quiet, and he is an inventor. He is always inventing something to make our work easier.

"You will really like Uncle Yaakoub. He is a storyteller. He loves to tell stories, especially funny ones. My father is the oldest brother, and he is the master potter of the Ra-eef' family. Although my older brother, Ranine, is really good. He will be the master potter someday."

"And your youngest brother is a slave to the Hebrews?"

"Yes. Keshub's freedom was the price Baba paid for wearing old clothes and worn-out sandals and for asking the Hebrews for a treaty. My father and the elders of Aijalon told Joshua they had come from a long distance to hear more about their God. In truth, Gibeon is but a hard day's walk from Gilgal. Our whole family and the others of Gibeon are slaves now. Joshua declared us woodcutters and water carriers for the Hebrews' house of god. But Joshua is a kind slave master to Keshub. I think my little brother is like Baba. He loves serving Joshua and learning about their god."

"Tell me again about the time you saw the bronze basin, with all its mirrors, in the Hebrew camp."

"I was spying from our perch, high above Jericho, when a shaft of the brightest light came from inside the curtained courtyard of the tabernacle. For a moment, instead of me being hidden from view and spying on the Hebrews, I felt I was blinded and found out. I had nowhere to hide. Keshub told me about the bronze basin with its mirrors later."

"Did he see it?"

"Oh, no. Only the Hebrews and mostly just the priests see it, when they are serving the God Most High in the tabernacle. Joshua spent most of every Sabbath reading from Moses's writings of the history of the Hebrew people. Keshub heard about the mirrored basin from Joshua's readings.

"Remember when you and I heard the old white owl in the pine tree at the dung gate? Just when we needed the guard to be frightened away from his post? I had a similar feeling that someone was watching us and helping us—even though I ... was not worthy of his notice."

* * *

Eskie waved at neighbor Aghtaan near ein el-Beled, Gibeon's major spring. He rounded the curve at the base of Gibeon's hill and led the donkeys to water. From the smaller spring, he could see the Ra-eef' guest house and the steps to the courtyard door. *Have I been away only these few days? It feels like a lifetime.*

Mando washed his face, hands, and arms, without being told. He lifted his tunic at the neck and dried his face, then swiped his hands on his hips. His eyes, big and round, searched the area. "How do I look?"

Eskie pretended a grimace. "Boy-dough, you look like the tousle-headed, underfed waif you are. My mamaa will love fattening you up. Never fear. You are welcome here. Let's tether the donkeys to the fence of the livestock pen, and ... go surprise them."

Shree-ee-yew!

... Eskie grinned and swallowed hard at the sound of muffled excitement stirring inside.

The door swung wide.

"Eskie!" Baba's deep voice boomed, and his wide smile and open arms drew Eskie into his embrace.

"It is good to be home, Baba. So much has happened," Eskie murmured into his father's neck.

Baba held him at arm's length and spoke with emotion. "Welcome home, son. We have been praying for you." The rest of Eskie's family ranged around them in the background.

Eskie drew back and swept his hand toward Mando. Baba's smile grew wider still, as he dipped his chin and his eyebrows shot up. "Who is this?"

Mando sidled up to Eskie and peeked out from behind.

Eskie cupped his hand at the back of the boy's head and directed him forward. "This is Mando from Jerusalem, nine harvests old, orphaned grandson of Zedek. I have adopted him as my little brother. He needs a family."

Mamaa came to Baba's side and reached to grasp Eskie's forearm. "Welcome home, son." Leaning her head in to see Mando better, she chirped, "Mando, there will be no problem making a place for a new son in this family. Come join the Ra-eef' men at dinner."

ᔥᐅᏹ

Hebrew camp at Hebron

Keshub stirred the lentil stew and laid the flat bread and the roasted mutton rations from the Asherite cooks on a warmed stone surrounded by hot coals. With the sun sinking near the horizon, daytime hot winds from the Sinai desert calmed. He fanned away a pesky sand fly and reached into a tuck in his girdle, withdrawing a fresh-picked stem of rosemary.

He rubbed his nose with the back of his hand, remembering Gran-mamaa sometimes called the scrubby bush *the crown of the hills*. Rolling a sizeable sprig between his palms, he transferred the oil to his exposed skin, from his ears to his ankles. He dropped the stem among the hot coals to fragrance their area and to ward off more flying pests.

"I see you have been busy, young man."

Keshub heard Mr. Phinehas before he saw him. "Yes, sir. Are you ready for your evening meal? I tried to keep it warm for you."

"That is thoughtful of you, Keshub. Joshua is fortunate to have you travel with him. You make me feel like I am at Gilgal with my family."

"Thank you, sir. Do you have a large family?" Keshub wondered about his own family at the evening meal in Gibeon … without him and without Eskie.

"Among the Hebrews, we are all family. For myself, I have four sons and three daughters. How long have you been in the Hebrew camp?"

"Since before wheat harvest. Almost three full moons now."

"I could tell your father has missed you very much. I enjoyed talking with him on the Sabbath in Aijalon Valley. Your father asked very good questions about the God Most High of the Hebrews. I wish all the sons of Abraham among God's chosen people would revere him as much as your father."

"Yes, sir. May I refill your water flask at the spring before it gets dark?"

"Excellent suggestion."

℠)℞

"Eskie?"

Eskie lay still on the rooftop sleeping quarters, gazing at the almost half moon shining down on them. "Yes?"

"Thank you ... big brother."

"You are welcome, sprout." Eskie drew a deep breath to say more, but a soft snore told him ... not tonight.

Sir. Thank you for my family. It is good to be home. Unable to sleep, Eskie rose from his bedroll. His feet whispered down the stone steps to the courtyard.

"Eskie?" Baba, leaned against the wall of the pottery yard, drinking a bedtime bowl of rosemary tea.

Eskie lowered himself to the steps next to him. "Sir?"

"You did not come home to stay, did you?"

"No, sir. I came home to let Mando experience a loving family and take back as many of the weapons from the battlefield as possible. ... And I need to learn from my wise baba all I can about the Hebrews I must face in a few days."

Baba nodded. "I could tell. Jerusalem has changed you."

Eskie leaned his elbows on his knees. He steepled his hands to rub the bridge of his nose. "Baba, I am different from when I left because then, I was simply your son and Sir Ghaleb's student. Since that time, I have met a girl who might become my wife someday, and I have become a soldier of the Jebusites. I have killed to protect my new friends, and I feel like an old man already. But I have become old without the experience and wisdom I need."

"Son. Recognizing your need for wisdom is the first step to becoming wise. I would say keep looking up. See the star, *the here-tofore and the hereafter*? There is a god who named that star. He *is* the God Most High of the Hebrews."

"Yes. I believe that, too. I am trying to learn patience—the patience I see in the God Most High."

Baba smiled. "Tell me what you have seen."

"All the days I spied from our perch above Jericho, I wondered why the Hebrews waited to cross the river. Waited to attack Jericho and so on. Then it occurred to me. If they had acted even one day sooner and if the battle in Aijalon Valley had happened earlier, the ripened wheat would have been beaten down. We would have had no harvest. Instead, we finished scything the wheat the day before the attack, and God fought the battle for us."

Baba reached his hand to Eskie's knee and his voice broke. "God Most High is already giving you wisdom, son." He lifted his eyes to the stars. "But of all God's qualities, patience might be the most difficult for any of us to achieve. ... Tomorrow is the Sabbath and no pottery work. Let's talk more under the big olive tree at the top of Gibeon's hill."

"[In] *the Negev* ... [Sabbath day of rest ...]," JOSHUA 10:40

Chapter 25
Father Abraham

Gibeon's Hill on the Sabbath   *Day 20*

Eskie folded his bedroll to a square and bent to clear rocks and pebbles from the place at his feet. He glanced below, where Mando and his new young cousins played hide-and-seek in and out the grape arbors, up and down the terraced steps. Times of quiet, followed by shrieks of delight. "Tell me, Baba, about Abraham, father of the Hebrews."

Baba leaned against the ancient olive tree and gazed toward the sun, risen only a hand's breadth from the horizon. "I am still mulling over all the son of the high priest told me. On that Sabbath day, Keshub and I went out to meet him at the rise above Aghtaan's olive grove. The same place Keshub and I met Joshua after he found out our lie.

"I asked him many questions. Mr. Phinehas quoted to me from the writings of Moses. He said God spoke to Abraham over four hundred years ago. God told Abraham he would make his descendants into a great nation and would bless them." Baba paused and raised an index finger from where it rested on his knee. "But hear this. God also said the nation would be a blessing to all people on earth. Those who bless the Hebrews, God will bless. Those who curse the Hebrews, God will curse."

Eskie picked up a small stone and threw it to strike a rock half-way to the hilltop cistern. "We have seen the curse part happen all around us. Kings Og, Sihon, Zedek, and all the others. Everyone who has gone out to destroy the Hebrews has been destroyed."

Baba stroked his bearded chin. "What about the Jebusites? What will they do?"

Eskie bowed his head with forearms on his knees. "First of all, they have done Joshua's work for him by hanging the Amorite Molech worshipers and murderers of their own people. It appears that the Jebusites were never Molech's followers—only unwilling serfs under Zedek's thumb. But now that they have taken over Jerusalem as their own, they will fight to the end, if attacked by Joshua's army. They are seeking a standoff. They will never give up, but they will honor a truce and be good neighbors, if Joshua's army marches on by."

"That is a bold plan, son. Where is Joshua's army now?"

Eskie straightened. "They have turned toward the Sinai and Egypt, though we do not believe they will leave Canaan."

"I am sure you are right." Baba raised a knee and propped an elbow. "God Most High promised Canaan to their father Abraham, according to Moses's writings. God told them they would be slaves in Egypt and return after four hundred years. They are here to set-tle this time."

Eskie snatched up a twig and scratched in the dirt. "We were all sure Joshua would direct his army to Jerusalem, after pursuing the five kings who attacked us here in Aijalon Valley. The battle at Debir was the fourth city of the five kings. Zedek's Jerusalem is the last of them. Instead, they turned to the Negev. Mr. Jozman said the cities near Beersheba are known for their abundant wheat harvests—reason enough for Joshua to head there next."

"Ah, Beersheba. Interesting."

Eskie snapped his head up. "What?"

"Mr. Phinehas said Father Abraham planted a tamarisk tree in Beersheba and 'called upon the name of the Lord, the Eternal God.'"

"Eternal? No beginning and no end?"

Baba smiled and leaned his head back to rest on the gnarled trunk. "Yes. *The heretofore and the hereafter,* the one who named the stars he created."

"Whoa. This God we are talking about gets bigger with everything we learn about him. He created the stars, he stopped the sun, ... and he directed the white owl when I needed his help." ...

...

Eskie paused, as Mando and Mattah scampered up the terrace stairs, chattering as if they had known each other forever. "Are you young mountain goats having fun?"

"Yes!" While breathless, Mando's forehead glistened with sweat, and his eyes sparkled with excitement. He and Mattah handed over two juglets of fresh, cool water from the spring. "Your mamaa sent us with this too—fresh figs we just picked on a ledge below."

"Thank you, brother."

Mando looked down, then back up, and whispered. "Thank you for bringing me here, Eskie."

Eskie nudged his shoulder with a fist. "You are welcome, Boy-dough."

When they turned and clattered down the stairs again, Eskie rubbed his nose. "Where were we before the he-goats arrived?"

Baba took another gulp of water. "Beersheba. Father Abraham lived there a long time and dug a well there, when the son of his old age was a youngster. Isaac was his name. Later Isaac would have twin sons. Esau, the older, is father of the Edomites down in the Arabah on the other end of the Salt Sea. The Hebrews are from twelve sons of Esau's brother, Jacob. They are the ones who went to

Egypt and became slaves, just as God had told Abraham.

"But, in Beersheba, it looked like Abraham's young son Isaac might not be the next generation God had promised."

"What happened in Beersheba?"

"God tested Abraham."

"What was the test?"

"God told Abraham to take his son, Isaac, to Moriah."

"Moriah? The mountain where Jerusalem spills down the side near the Gihon Spring?"

Baba nodded, looking away to the hills, where Jerusalem lay just over the horizon. A half day's brisk walk away. "God told Abraham to take Isaac to Moriah and to sacrifice him there as a burnt offering."

"What? Really? What did Abraham do?"

"He got up the next morning, chopped wood for the burnt offering, saddled his donkey, and set out with two servants and the boy."

Eskie wagged his head, with his mouth open.

Baba raised an eyebrow. "On the third day, Abraham arrived at Mount Moriah. He left his servants with his donkey and said, 'We will be back.'"

"He said 'we will be back'? So did Abraham not obey God?"

"No, he *did* obey."

"What happened then?"

Baba smiled. "Isaac carried the wood, not knowing he was meant to be the sacrifice. He asked, 'Father, where is the lamb for the burnt offering?' Abraham answered, 'God himself will provide the lamb, my son.'"

"What happened next?"

"They continued up Mount Moriah, probably to the highest point."

"Yes! I have been there, Baba. The highest point is a bald knob of limestone. An old Jebusite named 'Raunah has a threshing floor there now."

"Abraham built an altar of stones and placed the wood on it. He tied his son up." ... Baba's voice caught in his throat, and his hand came to his mouth. "Abraham laid his son on the wood. ... "

Eskie gripped his hands in his lap.

"And then he raised the knife to slay his son."

Eskie held his breath.

"But God spoke to Abraham from heaven. He said, 'Abraham!' And Abraham answered, 'Here I am.'" Then God said, 'Do not lay a hand on the boy. ... Now I know you fear God, because you have not withheld from me your son.'" Baba dried his eyes on the tail end of his girdle and tried to smile. "Eskie, when you have a son, you will understand better how hard it must have been for Abraham to even consider giving God the dearest thing he had."

Eskie blinked and swallowed hard.

"Then Abraham looked up, and there in a thicket was a ram caught by his horns."

Eskie leaned his head back and closed his eyes. "So just as Abraham said to Isaac, God provided the sacrifice ... and the both of them returned to the servants and the donkey."

* * *

At dinner time at the reed mat in the courtyard, Mamaa placed a large Ra-eef' bowl in the center. Cousin Rachel, brother Ranine's wife, passed flat bread. When the woven basket returned, Baba passed it over his shoulder and held his piece between his thumb and third finger. His index finger on top made a spoon.

Eskie and everyone else did the same—ready for Baba to dip first into the cold stew.

Baba raised his bread above his chin and closed his eyes. "God Most High, thank you for the bread we eat tonight and the stew prepared by gentle and capable hands. Thank you, God, for the Sabbath day you have made, for our family gathered around us, and for your merciful providence of this year's harvest. Watch over all my children—wherever they are tonight."

Baba reached to begin the meal, while Eskie caught his father's eye and raised his bread to salute the Ra-eef' master potter.

"So, Joshua subdued the whole region … [of] the Negev [including the cities of Arad, Hormah, and Beersheba]…" JOSHUA 10:40

Chapter 26
Murder at the Spring

Ra-eef' rooftop, Gibeon   *Day 21*

Eskie lay awake, taking in the familiar predawn harmony of Gibeon. Birds peeping in the grayness blended with soft snores near him. Just as he remembered when all five brothers occupied this same space. A proper rooster's crow sounded in the distance. Then came the smoky fragrance of last night's coals being stirred, with new tinder and kindling added.

Eskie turned back his homespun blanket, rocking to sit up. He yawned and stretched wide. Reaching for his sandals, he heard the courtyard door scrape. He glanced over the parapet. Baba's familiar form exited.

Eskie tied his rough-worn sandals on. He still needed to talk to Sanbar about a new pair.

Baba's voice. Raised in anger. At the spring.

Eskie rose and grabbed his girdle and gear.

"Eskie! Ranine!" Mamaa screamed.

He took the steps down in twos. Racing across the courtyard.

Grabbing his bronze sword with his right, he strong-armed the gate open with his left and dashed down the steps. At the bottom, the spring came into view in dim light. A dark hulking figure raised a hand …

Eskie racing to help. "No!"

The venom of a dagger.

A gasp of surrender.

A scream behind him. "Ish-ta-ba!"

Eskie too late. Ire of gripping fury exploding within. He grasped the shoulder of the attacker and slung him away.

Reeling backward, the assailant growled with gritted teeth.

Eskie tensed to pursue.

"Eskie, help me! Baba is hurt!"

The attacker fled to Aghtaan's olive grove.

Eskie halted. Baba needed him. He turned back. Kneeling beside Baba and using Baba's girdle to stanch the flow of blood.

Baba lay still. His face an unnatural color.

Ranine appeared. Barefoot.

Mamaa knelt on Baba's other side. She cooed, "Ishtaba? Ishtaba?"

Baba groaned—a deep, powerless sound.

"Boys," came Mamaa's voice, soft, firm, as she rose. "We must move him inside. Carry him as gently as you can. I will make a pallet in the courtyard."

Eskie still kneeling—helpless, looked up at Ranine, frozen.

Uncle Samir arrived and knelt. "Eskie." He clasped his left hand to his right forearm. "Slowly, gently."

Eskie mirrored his uncle and slipped his right arm under Baba's neck and grasped Samir's forearm.

Samir found Eskie's left forearm. "Take his feet, Ranine."

"Get your balance, men. We lift him slowly … and gently … keeping his head up."

Uncle Samir's soft words helped calm the burning anger within him. Eskie willed himself to think only of taking careful moves to the entrance ... up the steps ... through the door, swung wide. Held by Mando and Mattah ... eyes as big as ripe figs.

"Over here!" Mamaa made a place by the kitchen fire.

"Slow. Steady." Uncle Samir guided their steps, while Eskie's feet felt like blocks of limestone. He knelt, lowering Baba and gauging his movements to match his uncle's—though his blood raced within him.

"Ishtaba, stay with us," Mamaa whispered, as she pressed clean cloths to Baba's wound.

Uncle Samir felt his brother's wrist. "Eskie, press the cloths harder to Ishtaba's wound."

Mamaa lifting away a red-soaked rag, added another.

Eskie pressed hard. The rhythmic throb at the wound pushed back. "Baba. Do not go. Please."

Lips clamped between his teeth, Samir spread a blanket from Baba's feet to his waist. Then checked his pulse again, his brows coming together in dismay.

Mamaa stroked Baba's forehead. "Ishtaba, we love you."

The family filled the courtyard. Hushed voices in the background. Soft sobs.

... Eskie felt less strength in each throb.

Baba's sunburned skin took on the color of ashes in a cold campfire.

Mamaa bent low, spoke near his ear. "Ishtaba." Her voice caught. She gulped. "If you must go, we will be all right."

The creases on his forehead relaxed. ... A faint smile.

Eskie met Uncle Samir's gaze.

He moved his head slowly, side to side.

Mamaa combed Baba's thick hair with her fingers. "A good husband. ... A good father." She caressed his jaw. ... "A good, good man."

...

Eskie leaned back on his heels and covered his face with his hands. A leering, growling face taunted him. He stood, clenched his hands at his side, and pivoted to the courtyard door. *I have to get out of here. How could this happen? One day, he taught me about wisdom and patience. Now the next, he is gone? God, how can this be?*

Eskie slammed the door behind him and strode to the spring. On his knees, he splashed water in his face. He beat the ground. Desperate. Crying out. *God, I needed more time with Baba.*

...

Ranine's sandaled feet appeared beside him. ... Joined by Uncles Samir and Yaakoub.

Yaakoub leaned on crutches and barely raised his voice. "Did you see who did this, Eskie?"

... "Ragar." To say his name brought bitter gall to his mouth. ... Eskie rose to his feet. Burning anger from the depth of his being threatened to take hold of him. He needed to feel Ra-eef's strength of character and integrity around him. He needed Baba, but Uncle Yaakoub and Uncle Samir would be the next best thing. He embraced them both at once and clung tight, drawing on the essence of their strength to sustain him.

From his uncles, Eskie turned to his brothers Ranine and Rami, drawing them together, foreheads touching. He whispered, "We have big sandals to fill, but the creator God and Star Namer will help us. Right?"

Eyes streaming, they stepped back.

Eskie cleared his throat. "I need to track Ragar in Aghtaan's orchard. As soon as possible."

Uncle Yaakoub took charge. "First, every one of us must be armed immediately. Ranine, bring out the cache of swords and daggers from the pottery yard. Rami, get yours and run the short-cut to tell Ya-yah' and La'ana what has happened. I will guard the courtyard. Samir, go with Eskie. The two of you should get supplies from Raga in the kitchen, since you do not know how long you will be out pursuing that demon."Ranine, alert the village and Sir Ghaleb. He will no doubt send men into the orchard from the other side and runners to the other cities of Aijalon. They must send a team to the wood camp. Let's hope Ragar slunk away in the night, instead of massacring the others in their sleep. Regardless, they need to know what has happened, and they need a new team.

"Eskie, Ranine, let's say if you have not found Ragar's tracks in the orchard by noon, all the searchers should meet at ein el-Beled to consider what to do next."

Eskie marveled at the deep gravelly voice of his uncle. Unlike in his storytelling mode, the voice of his uncle sounded more like Baba than Eskie had ever realized.

* * *

Geared up and at their small spring within sight of the livestock pen, Eskie met Mando and Mattah, both lugging yokes of water. "Thank you, Mattah, for including Mando today in your chores."

"Aw, we are glad he is here. Only thing is, it is a little confusing. Is he my uncle or my cousin?"

Eskie tousled Mattah's hair. "We three are all grandsons of Ra-eef' the potter, so that makes you and Lehab our cousins. Mando and I are brothers." Eskie put a fist to Mando's shoulder.

Mattah wagged his head. "See. I told you so."

"Aw. There are so many names here for me to learn." Mando shrugged.

"Hey, squirt. I will be away hunting for Ragar. You stay here until I come for you."

* * *

Eskie shouldered his knapsack and led the way. "Ragar ran that way, but let's look for footprints around the spring. Maybe he hid behind the reeds here, waiting for a Ra-eef' to appear. Did it have to be Baba? He does not always go to the spring in the mornings."

Samir shook his head. "I still cannot believe this happened."

"Here is a footprint."

"Ragar's?"

"It is big. On the backside, away from the courtyard."

"Ten days or so since we had a caravan camping near here."

Eskie scratched the back of his head. "It has to be Ragar's, then. ... See this gouge in the left heel?"

"We have not had rain in weeks, so we will not see any more prints in mud."

"Then you taught me to look more carefully for freshly over-turned rocks and impressions in sandy areas. I will take the left, and we will angle this way to the orchard." Eskie scanned the rocky soil with extra care at a dusty trail crossing Ragar's path. But no. A flock going out to pasture already ¬¬this morning erased any clues.

Samir called out. A fresh footprint. Surely Ragar's.

Eskie inspected it. Nodded and continued. Silent now, he listened for clues. ... He motioned for Samir to come closer. He pointed to a rosemary seedling broken off at the base, a partial print with it. No heel visible, but probably Ragar's, from the fresh scent wafting up. ... *We must now keep our noses to the air.* He whispered, "How is your sense of smell? If we get close enough for him to jump us, we might smell rosemary."

Samir nodded.

Eskie adjusted the angle to enter the orchard in line with the last footprint. *Unlikely to find rosemary growing in the shade of olive trees. If there is rosemary smell here, there will be Ragar. Sir. Help us find him.* Zigzagging through olive trees, he swiveled his head left and right and bobbed up and down, to inspect the ground and foreground.

Samir halted.

Eskie sucked in a breath, on alert.

Samir rubbed his forefinger under his nose.

Rosemary.

Samir trod with care toward a rock big enough to hide behind.

Eskie circled wide, choosing his steps for silence—he hoped. He smelled rosemary, too.

Samir lunged to crest the rock.

Eskie flanked it. ... Vacant. No one there. "But look." He pointed toward home. From there, Ragar would have seen everything that happened at the spring after Eskie chased him away.

Samir nodded.

Eskie found another print among the soft sand of an ant lion colony. He pointed.

Samir lifted his chin, agreeing.

How long did he watch us? He might be close by. Eskie widened his parallel path with his uncle. They approached the far side of Aghtaan's grove of trees, halfway to the ridgeline trail.

* * *

Coming out of the orchard, Eskie stopped.

Samir closed the gap between them, searching for any new prints exiting the orchard, and found one. He pointed and squatted, with one knee down.

Eskie lined up behind his young uncle—the print pointing to the rocky incline. "Did he forge ahead to the ridgeline trail? At the ridgeline, he would be on a beeline to Jerusalem."

"You think he would go to Jerusalem?"

"I do not know. I know his brother is there. Ragar does not know Dagan is there too—with his brother."

Samir raised his eyebrows. "Tell me about that later. Which way now?"

"If he went back to the village, Sir Ghaleb's men will likely find him. So let's take the high road to Jerusalem."

Samir nodded and took a swig from his water flask.

Eskie, too, and he reached in his knapsack for two dried figs. Offering one, he popped his in. "This way."

* * *

Sir, we have seen enough partial footprints to believe we are still trailing Ragar. Help us catch up with him before he reaches the livery stable. Please, God.

"Joshua subdued the whole region ... [of] the Negev." Joshua 10:40

Chapter 27
Ragar and the Liveryman

On the ridgeline trail near Jerusalem   *Continuing Day 21*

"Nearly midday already, can we jog? We need to catch up with Ragar, or at least get there before dark." Eskie swiped his brow with the back of his hand.

"So you think I am getting old and flabby, nephew? You spent so much time spying in that little perch above Jericho you will be the slow one." Samir sprinted ahead ten paces and settled into a jog.

Eskie laughed to see him use the same trick his son Lehab often used. *The pomegranate does not fall far from the bush.* He caught up with his longtime mentor in charge of gathering wood for firing days in the pottery yard. "That is where you are wrong, Unk. That job was so boring I jogged in place at least four times a day just to keep awake." Eskie tipped up his water flask.

"Hunh. Top of next hill. All out. Prove it." Samir loped down the hill, with no warning.

Eskie caught him halfway up the next hill and pulled ahead three paces, before they reached the top. Hands on his knees, he surveyed the trail ahead, breathing hard. To Samir when he caught up, "You are not too bad for an old goat with five kids."

"It is always the inexperienced young bucks who butt heads to compete."

Eskie laughed … and grabbed his head and sobbed. "Why, Samir? Why did Baba die?"

Samir wrapped his arms around his nephew and best friend and rocked back and forth. "I am asking the same question, man."

* * *

Past midafternoon, Eskie pointed down to the wadi of the cheesemakers' valley and the bend at the livery stable, where the almost-dry stream trickled into the Bin-Hinnom.

Samir pointed, too. "Is that Ragar on that ledge behind the house?"

Eskie confirmed. "That is him. Probably waiting for sundown. What if we split up? You go on down the trail and tell Rangon what is happening. Ragar might not recognize you walking alone."

"Sure. What will you do?"

"I am going into Jerusalem by the back way to get help. Big Jebusite stonemasons and timbermen is what I have in mind. Ragar is as strong as an ox from wielding an ax all day for several moons now."

"I was wondering how you and I could do this. Hurry, man. You know what they say about a cornered rat."

Eskie leveled a knowing gaze. "Exactly." *Sir. All afternoon I have asked for help. I am asking again—for help in bringing Ragar to justice. But, Lord, I do not understand why Baba had to die today.*

* * *

Running for the back entrance to Jerusalem, Eskie slowed to a walk, passing 'Raunah's threshing floor. He visualized Baba's tale, no, Moses's tale of Abraham bringing his son here. Abraham obeyed the God of heaven who spoke to him—even to the point of raising his knife. What faith! He promised 'we will be back' and 'God himself will provide a sacrifice.' *Did he think God would bring his son to life again? Thank you, God, for the time I had to learn from Baba. Thank you for Baba's time with the high priest's son. Thank you, God, that you brought Ragar here so we could get help from the Jebusites.*

* * *

Eskie slid to a stop at Jozman's conference-room door. He stepped into the doorway and bowed slightly, seeking entrance.

"Eskie! We were just talking about you … What is wrong? What has happened?" Jozman rose to his feet.

Eskie shook his head to clear his thoughts and used the tail of his girdle to mop his eyes.

"Sir, I need …." Blinking, he tried to clear his throat. "…your help."

"Tell me what has happened."

* * *

Please, God, let no one else get hurt by this madman. Eskie slipped out the main gate of Jerusalem into twilight shadow. The sun drained behind the rim of the mountain beyond the livery, cloaking Rangon's house in advancing darkness. He waved the four stonemasons to descend into the bin-Hinnom, where they would approach the livery from below view.

Ragar has had all afternoon to plan his moves. Help us, God.

Nearing the livery, Eskie's being cried out at the eerie silence magnified by the buzzing of bees at the hive in the cassia tree.

"Rangon! Dagan!" Not a sound in reply. His heart leapt to his throat. *Surely not, surely not. ...* He entered the livestock pen—unsheathing his dagger. He sidestepped to see past the cassia tree on the far side of the house. The timbermen would come from the drop-off to the cheesemakers' wadi there. *Soon, I hope.*

He angled back to the near side and ran an undulating hand along the smooth coat of a back and rump of a donkey in his path. He glanced past the ladder to the rooftop. Stonemasons came into view from the Hinnom. He dared not signal but took slow, cautious steps. They stopped, warned and alert. *Good men. Help us, God.*

He peered into the darkness of the stone house. "Rangon?"

"Well, well. We have another high-and-mighty Ra-eef' coming to call, Rangon." Easing into light from the edge of shadow, Ragar appeared unused to smiling and his voice unpracticed in niceties. His features snapped back to grotesque hatred and a guttural growl. "Stop right there, oh privileged one of Gibeon."

"Where is Samir?"

"Your young uncle? Oh, he is right here ... waiting for you."

Eskie sucked in breath—his eyes following Ragar's careful setup. At the doorway, his right foot tucked behind one leg of a small stool. On it, a heavy basalt anvil rested half on, half off, with a rope around its middle. The rope ran taut to the midceiling support log. ... The other end, also taut, ended around Samir's neck.

Eskie dipped his chin and swallowed. *God, help.*

"You see, son of the self-righteous potter, I have the upper hand here." His eyes glowed like the night fires of bin-Hinnom. His left hand clasped an Amorite dagger.

Eskie flinched.

"Yes. You recognize the cook's butcher's knife you gave him. Pity. With all his stories of *serving the king*, all he served me—was slop." His nostrils flared, as he gritted his teeth and snarled. "When you rush me to save your old uncle, I will kick the table, hang him, and gut you."

Eskie clamped his lips in his teeth and slanted his mouth to the side. *What can I do? Are the stonemasons ready on the left? Are the timbermen in place on the right?* He dared not focus on them, lest he set Ragar's plan into motion. Eyes locked with Ragar's, he spoke in a monotone, "Are you sure your plan will work? Perhaps that old rope is rotten. Is the ceiling rafter strong enough? What about Rangon and his son?"

"Oh, I have not decided yet. They are tied up inside, sniveling weaklings."

"What about Dagan, your own son?"

"Is he?"

"What do you mean?" Eskie kept his voice even, calm.

"I mean, do I really *know* I am the father of that doormat? Ketzia left me saddled with the squalling brat, but am I really the father?"

Eskie controlled his disgust. "Ragar, what is it you want from all this?"

"Satisfaction. I will have the greatest day of my life today. I will rid Canaan of not one, but three of your clan. And I will be the Amorite who makes the pottery weaklings rue the day they rejected Adoni-Zedek's help. Proud fools. All of you!" Seething with rage, Ragar glared and gritted his teeth, shaking his shaggy head.

Eskie lunged, with his dagger extended.

Ragar dodged the blade and shifted to upend the stool.

A stonemason leapt high to grasp the rope and steady the anvil. Another dove in low to stop the movement of the small table.

Eskie jumped to avoid massive, flailing legs.

Livid with rage, Ragar slashed with wild thrusts of his butcher's knife.

A timberman, springing out, chopped, severing Ragar's extended wrist.

Ragar's unbridled scream! Staring at spurting blood. Grabbing his forearm tight at midway, kicking out at the first timberman. Turning and backing away toward the wadi.

"You cannot escape, Ragar. That arm, left untended, will bleed you out before the moon rises." Eskie advanced.

Jebusites flanked him. Crunching step for step.

"You have nowhere to go, Ragar." Another step forward.

Ragar slunk backward, eyes darting side to side. More blood, dripping fast.

Rangon appeared at Eskie's side. "Give yourself up, brother. Get help with that arm."

Ragar sneered, eyes filled with fear. "What good would I be with one arm?"

"What good did you choose to be with two strong arms, little brother?" Rangon's quiet voice held no condemnation.

Eskie took a quick step.

Ragar turned and ran ... straight into the cassia tree.

A cloud of angry bees swarmed. Attacking.

Ragar lost his grip on his arm. One hand clawing at his head. ... Blood gushing.

Eskie stepped back in horror. Bees prevented any offer of aid.

Writhing in the dirt. ... Screaming. ... Ragar went limp. Eyes staring.

Eskie gulped—feeling no satisfaction. *Two very different men died today.*

* * *

Samir brought a lantern holding a candle.

Rangon knelt beside his brother.

Eskie found Dagan shaking with sobs and hiding his face against the side of the liveryman's house. Eskie placed an arm across the boy's shoulders. "Do you want to see your father?"

"Why? He claimed I am not his son. That would explain all the abuse I have taken from him. Right? I would rather leave it at that. Maybe I will not hate him as much that way. The rejection and the hatred have eaten at me my whole life."

… Eskie sighed, "I am sorry, friend."

Dagan tensed. "You can call me friend, after this?"

"Yes, I can. You are not your father."

"What if I am like my father?"

"Every person makes his own choices. Choose good, Dagan."

Eskie lifted his eyes to brilliant starlight, beginning at the dim outline of the Hill of Evil Counsel before him. Outshining them all, Baba's favorite star twinkled its message of hope. The namer of the stars—*the Eternal One*—cares.

"[Joshua] *totally destroyed ...* [the Negev] *just as the Lord ...
had commanded."* JOSHUA 10:40

Chapter 28
Where Is the Enemy Now?

Jerusalem, three days later   *Day 24*

"Eskie, are those new sandals?" Rangon bent over his work-bench, repairing a bridle.

Eskie sucked in a deep breath. "Yes. The last pair my father made before he died." He cleared his throat. *Will it begin to hurt less to say that?*

Rangon ducked his head. "I am sorry, man."

Eskie nodded. "I am sorry we arrived so late last night and slept so late this morning. I need to report to Mr. Jozman this morning, but Mando is still snoring up there."

"Not anymore." Mando's head popped up above the parapet. "I will be down quick as a wink—after I roll up my new bedroll from Mamaa Danya." His smile spread from ear to ear.

Eskie marveled at the difference in the lad since his acceptance by all the family in Gibeon. *My mother ... and father truly welcomed him with open arms.* Eskie swiped his nose with his thumb and retrieved the knapsack and donkey packs he stowed last night under the lean-to at the back of Rangon's house.

"I have hot peppermint tea." Rango waved from the cook fire.

"And Mando and I have gifts for everyone."

"Gifts?" Rangon dipped his chin and tilted his head.

Eskie held patched linen bags. "From Mamaa to Rangon, dried apricots and a bag of wheat, both this year's crop. Mamaa is afraid I might eat too much here and wear out my welcome."

"Never." Rangon took his bags and sniffed, waggling his eyebrows.

Whe—eet! Eskie whistled. "Dagan, come over here. I have something for you."

Hesitant, Dagan came and leaned his hay fork on the house. "For me?"

"Yes. My mother has been weaving and sewing her new-season flax cloth. The last time she saw you in Gibeon, she thought you were growing out of your old tunic."

Mando dropped down from the ladder's last rung. "I got one, too! Not even handed down … a little itchy, though." He squirmed his shoulders inside the new linen.

"Ah. You will get used to it, but it does make you appreciate a garment already broken in by someone else." Eskie brought out a larger bag, with oddly shaped contents. "And this is for you, Rango. Here, open it."

Rango frowned. "For me?"

"Yes. This contraption is from Uncle Samir."

Rango stammered. "Samir? Who was here? I only met him that once. Why?"

"This is his specialty—figuring things out … to work better. Let's see it."

Rango did his crippled-man crawl away from the fire and reached for the linen bag. Out fell a crutch and a short, sturdy stick, with leather and straps attached to one end.

Eskie stepped to Rango's right side. "Dagan, help me get Rango up on his good leg."

From Rango: "No, man. I cannot do that."

"Let's try." Eskie motioned to Mando. "Here, hold the crutch until we need it."

Rango trembled.

"Uncle Samir said your leg is still good from the knee up. Mando?" Eskie supported Rango's right forearm, and Mando inserted the crutch under Rango's arm.

Eskie loosened his hole but hovered in place. "How does that feel?"

"Not too bad, but I cannot put weight on that foot."

"Yes. Not on the foot, but on the knee. Bend your knee and rest it on this leather cradle. It has padding inside a pocket here, and I will strap it on like a sandal, here … and here." Eskie stepped back, but within reach. "Now put your weight on your knee. How is that?"

"Not bad. I think I can get used to it." A broad grin broke out. "It is better than crawling in the dirt, for sure."

"Great. And Mamaa sent you Mando's old tunic, washed of course. If your armpit or knee gets sore, fold this and use it for padding."

Rango struggled to speak. "I do not know how to thank you enough, man."

Eskie shook his head. "Samir hoped it would help."

* * *

Eskie heard the Jebusite conference in progress, before he appeared at the door.

All conversation halted. Jebus rose and greeted him cheek to cheek. "I was so sorry to hear about your father, Eskie. He was such a good, brave man. Both times I was in his presence, he told Zedek no in such a strong, quiet way that Zedek was flummoxed. I was inspired by your father's rock-hard strength of character."

Eskie nodded. "Thank you, Jebus, for your kind words."

Jozman stood behind Jebus and stepped up. "Perhaps you should not have come back, Eskie. But we are glad you did."

🕰

Hebrew camp at Hebron

Keshub shifted the yoke of water jars on his shoulders, as he wove through lines of wagons loaded for travel. "Sir, where do you want this water?"

"Here beside me."

Keshub bent to settle the round-bottom clay jars among rocks already prepared as props.

Mr. Phinehas brought from his personal wagon two large, bronze bowls, with golden cords attached, and a small, bronze box. "Keshub, stand holding your yoke in place, while I attach these bowls." He dipped from the water jars and poured. *"Let the heart of them rejoice ... seek his face evermore. ..."* Filling both bronze bowls near to full, he laid down the dipper.

"... Now I am adding, according to Moses's instructions, a pinch of ashes from the sacrifice of an unblemished red heifer to make water of cleansing." The high priest's son took up a bundle of hyssop, tied with a red cord. "Follow me."

Keshub chose his gait and his steps to keep the blessed water from sloshing out. He followed behind, as Mr. Phinehas stopped and sprinkled each wagon loaded for transport and murmured, *"Bless the Lord, O my soul. ... O give thanks unto the Lord. ... Call upon his name, make known his deeds among the people. ... Talk ye of all his wondrous works. Glory in his holy name. ... Let the heart of them rejoice that seek the Lord. Seek the Lord, and his strength. ..."*

Seek his face evermore. Remember his marvelous works that he hath done ... his wonders, and the judgments of his mouth. O ye seed of Abraham his servant, ye children of Jacob his chosen. He is the Lord our God ... His judgments are in all the earth."

Keshub, bowed by the yoke across his shoulders, lowered his eyes, too. To hear the priest's recitation of the goodness of the Hebrew god moved him.

From the wagons, Mr. Phinehas turned to the packs—lined up and ready to be lifted into place on a donkey or a camel for the next journey. Repeating his words of praise to God, he sprinkled each one.

Keshub sensed the lightening of his burden. He followed along, speaking the words of Phinehas in his heart.

Near his wagon again, Mr. Phinehas turned. "Keshub, we have received word from Joshua. All the army will arrive today. We will be going back to Gilgal tomorrow."

Tomorrow! What about Jerusalem?

՚ॐঌ

On Mount Moriah, in the olive grove near Jerusalem

"Eskie, how do you figure that timing again? Are we sure this time Joshua will arrive tomorrow?" one of the best Jebusite long-bow archers queried from among the group.

Another spoke up, "We *have* thought that before."

From the back, one of them interrupted, "And it did not happen."

Eskie took a step forward. "You are right men. The obvious answer is none of us can *know* the future without a doubt. But we have word from the Bedouin runners Joshua is definitely headed to Hebron today. When they arrive there, will they tarry for the night or a day? I think *not* for a day, and perhaps not for the night, either. If they stop, they could not be in Gilgal before their Sabbath day of rest begins.

"Will they start from Hebron tomorrow and reach Jerusalem tomorrow late in the day? Possibly. ... Or will the high priest's son waiting for Joshua at Hebron have all the wagons, carts, camels, and donkeys they have acquired loaded and ready? I think it is highly possible as soon as Joshua arrives to provide an armed guard and as soon as the full moon rises, they will move toward Jerusalem."

Eskie steepled his hands and rubbed the tip of his nose. "Their first units could be here at daybreak tomorrow. Especially if they do not stay with the stuff, but quick march for a surprise attack. They have done this before. From here, they can go to their home camp at Gilgal on the day after tomorrow and arrive before their every-seventh-day Sabbath, which begins at sundown."

The men showed grim acceptance of his assessment of the situation.

Jebus clasped an arm across Eskie's back. "Tonight, Jozman, Eskie, and I will lay our bedrolls on a rooftop in En-Rogel so we can meet Joshua first—whenever he arrives. You men will spend the night in the marketplace plaza at Gihon Spring.

"I will send a flaming arrow into the bin-Hinnom, night or day, when they arrive. Two, if they appear to rush an attack. That will be your signal to rouse all the other archers to take their positions on the wall, and you will take your places on the tower."

Jozman joined Eskie on his other side. "Do you have any questions?" ... With none, he turned. "Eskie, what is it your father always said?"

Eskie cleared his throat. "We prepare for what we can prepare for. We face with integrity what we cannot prepare for."

"All these kings and their lands Joshua conquered in one campaign, because the Lord, the God of Israel, fought for Israel." JOSHUA 10:42

Chapter 29
Confronting the Enemy

Jerusalem   Day 25

Eskie settled in for first watch and grinned at Jozman, snoring in the corner like a piglet in a pea patch. He stared into the starlit darkness toward Hebron and lifted his eyes to Baba's star. "Jebus, do you know the ancient name of that star above the Hill of Evil Counsel?"

"No. Do you?"

"My gran-baba learned the name as a lad. An old, wise man told the story of the ages written in the stars. The name of that star, in particular, intrigued him."

"What is the name?"

"The heretofore and the hereafter."

"What happened before and what will happen after today?"

"Yes."

"Are you thinking that star has seen what has happened before and knows what is coming?"

"No. Not the star. The one who named the star. Maybe the one who named that star is beyond that star and beyond our understanding. The father of the Hebrews called him the Eternal God."

"No beginning and no end?"

"That is right. Maybe the One who named the star stands beyond the heavens and sees everything that came before and everything that will come hereafter."

"That would be a very big god, indeed, friend."

"What if he were even bigger than that?"

"What could be bigger than that?"

Eskie scratched the back of his head. "What if he could see it all at once? All that has gone before, and all that will come after. All in the star namer's view … at once."

Z-z-z-z-z.

Across the way, dark shadows crossed to and fro in front of a campfire beside Gihon Spring. Eskie whispered, *"Lord Eternal, you promised to bless those who bless your chosen people. Help us … bless the Hebrews tomorrow. We seek your blessing on the city of Jerusalem and the Jebusites.*

* * *

"Eskie!" Baba called his name. He ran down the terraced stairs in new sandals Baba made. …

"Eskie!"

"Wha-at?" His dream faded, as Jebus shook his shoulder again.

"Come look. They are here."

Rolling out of his bedroll—alert. "How close? Where? It is still quite dark." He came along Jebus at the parapet. "How can you tell?"

"Look at the nearest hill across the valley. Watch closely. They have one lantern at the front of the line."

Eskie shook his head, remembering Keshub's account of Joshua's arrival in Aijalon Valley. "If the larger army is that close, check every tree or small outcropping between there and here. The advance unit may be closer. How long before the sun's rising?"

Jebus checked the horizon toward the Jordan River. "The sun will be up before they arrive, but not long before. I will shoot the arrow and keep watch here. You must warn the old man down below and send his son across the Kidron to clarify to the others the enemy may launch an attack at any moment."

* * *

Moments before sunshine would flood the valley below, Eskie raised a lighted torch. Signaling to the lantern-led line of foot soldiers in the valley below, "We know you are coming." He made a perfect target for the enemy closer to him, but he could not see them—yet. He held a drawn sword at attention, with hilt over his heart. Beside him, Jozman held a javelin, with a white flag fluttering in the morning breeze.

Jebus, beside Jozman, held the longest bow Eskie had ever seen. Indeed, his friend knew how to use the long-range weapon with strength and skill. Although, for now, the tip rested on the ground before him. If Eskie's plan worked, Jebus would draw the bowstring only for demonstration. If the plan did not work—*God help us all.*

...

Eskie recognized Joshua marching up the incline, surrounded by six personal bodyguards. Men of the first unit rose from their shadowed hiding places, as he came abreast of them. They followed behind, flanking him—arrows nocked in place but held at their sides.

Jozman stepped forward three paces—his white hair glowing in the early-morning light.

Joshua's bodyguard slowed. From all around, the first unit stood, revealing their hiding places.

Joshua kept his pace ... and drew near.

Jozman bowed at the waist. "Welcome, gentlemen, to the city whose name means peace. All men of integrity and peace are welcome here."

Joshua lowered his chin, his deep voice carrying far. "Integrity and peace are noble goals for all men. What happened to the descendants of Zedek, the Amorite king of Jerusalem who attacked Gibeon?"

Jozman bowed at the waist again. "They are no more, sir. We Jebusites have taken hold of Jerusalem to rule in honor and decency ... and integrity."

Eskie stepped forward to join Jozman. "Sir, I am Gibeonite. Eskie, third son of Ishtaba, the ... master potter of Gibeon."

Joshua's brows arched high. "We have met."

"Yes, sir. Your servant, Keshub, is my brother. May I speak for the Jebusites, sir?"

Joshua glanced at Jozman with his white hair and dipped his chin.

Jozman nodded his consent.

Joshua returned his gaze to Eskie.

"Sir, these men hanged Zedek's son and his followers of Molech on the tower they built to sacrifice young children. Only men of integrity lead the stalwarts of the Jebusites. They desire to live in peace with the Hebrews, but they are prepared to fight to their death for this small piece of Canaan."

Joshua raised one eyebrow.

Eskie raised an eyebrow, too. "If I may be so bold, sir, I would say you have done a service to the land of Canaan by cleansing this land of the murderers of babies in the fires of Molech. You are nearing your home camp in Gilgal, sir. I would suggest your men are anxious to sit at their home fires with their families. We have gifts for your homecoming. We wish you well."

Joshua opened his mouth to speak.

Eskie hurried on. "Sir, if you and your guards would care to see

Jerusalem from this vantage point, I invite you this way."

Joshua and his squad of six came forward.

Eskie and Jebus turned with them. "You see, sir, if you think your first unit could storm the walls of Jerusalem and walk away with the gem of Canaan, I show you the price you will have to pay. Jebus, demonstrate your marksmanship on that target yonder halfway up the bin-Hinnom Valley."

Jebus stepped forward to the crest of the pass into the Kidron Valley, raised his bow, and inserted his arrow. The muscles of his arms and chest bulged beneath his linen tunic, as he pulled. He released with a whisper and *zing*. The arrow arched into the air and zeroed into the center circle of the target.

Complete silence.

Eskie allowed the realization to sink in that here and now they were within range of the longbow archers on the tower across the way.

Eskie glanced at Joshua, whose mouth hung slightly ajar. He continued with a soft voice. "Sir, all the men you see on the tower at the main gate have longbows and are equally skilled. The others you see manning the wall all the way around Jerusalem have regular bows and arrows. But the Jebusite craftsmen make the best and truest of arrows. What they aim at, they hit. Your first unit would suffer major casualties like you have not experienced before in all Canaan.

"Mr. Phinehas, the son of your high priest, told my father Ishtaba about your father Abraham. He said God chose your people and promised to bless your people—and anyone else who chose to bless you."

Eskie bent low at the waist and straightened. "Sir. We, the unchosen, wish to learn of your god. We wish to be neighbors and bless your people. We wish to live at peace with you. What say you?"

Joshua's frowning, rugged face, with deep, leathery creases, cracked open with a smile of bright pearls. "Is that all?"

Eskie stood speechless. "Sir?"

"You present a convincing argument. And my men are pawing the dirt to return to Gilgal for sure."

Jozman cleared his throat. "Sir, we have a feast prepared for your first unit, as you wait for those who follow behind to catch up. If you would care to partake, we will finish setting up and be ready to serve you quickly." He raised his brows, questioning.

Joshua smiled again. "Certainly. God has prepared a table for us by the hands of our enemies. Thank you. We accept."

"Give us a few moments, sir." Jozman lifted his javelin high and laid it down at his feet.

The Jebusites on the wall of Jerusalem sent out a hearty cheer.

The steward of the kitchen, with all the old men of the Jebusites, streamed out the main gate. They carried trays laden with food and headed to booths already set up in the Kidron Valley.

All the archers rested their bows on the wall before them but held an arrow over their heart—ready at a moment's notice, if called to arms.

Eskie stood back and smiled, as the golden-bearded lion faces of the first unit filed into the Kidron Valley. The same men who had led the rescue of his family at the battle for Gibeon.

Joshua came to stand beside him, watching his men go by. "Eskie, right?"

"Yes, sir."

Joshua gave him a sidewise glance and smiled a crooked smile. "So Keshub is the quiet one, right?"

Eskie bit his tongue and nodded.

"... Then Joshua returned with all Israel to the camp at Gilgal. [...
in time to observe the Sabbath.]" JOSHUA 10:43

Epilogue

The Kidron Valley   *Day 25*

Still early in the day, Eskie kept alert for any sign of trouble. He followed step for step three paces behind Jozman. Every fourth step, a Jebusite archer on the tower and wall of Jerusalem aimed his arrow at Joshua, until he passed. Eskie would be anxious being near their target, if he did not have confidence in their marksmanship.

Jozman escorted Joshua to the feast prepared for the invaders. The leader of the Jebusites regaled the leader of the invaders with the diligence and industry of his people.

Joshua wiped his hands on the end of his girdle, accepted a portion of roasted lamb wrapped in fresh grape leaves, and glanced at Eskie. He nodded to the old man who served him—with an Amorite dagger tucked in his girdle. Joshua's smile did not waver.

Eskie exhaled an unspoken prayer. *Lord, please allow us to serve the Hebrews this hospitality without any conflict.*

Next, Jozman led them to the line of vendors' carts on down the Kidron and explained, with a bow, "Sir, if you think you have time, our people have assembled a few gifts your men can take home—

perhaps to their loved ones. Here, we have child-size wooden toys, rag dollies, hair ribbons, small pouches, clay toy dishes, or condiment bowls. And here we have olive oil soap. We hope there are enough individual items that all your men can take something."

"Quite a nice selection. Thank you for your thoughtfulness. Especially the olive oil soap." Joshua's eyes twinkled, as he selected a palm-size bar. "A good bath in the Jordan River sounds like a dream today."

Jozman stopped at the beginning of the line of booths to explain the soldiers got only one choice.

Eskie stayed in step with Joshua and his bodyguard.

"Children's toys here!"

"Olive oil soap over here!"

"Ladies' baubles here!"

"Pickled duck's eggs, while they last!"

Joshua rocked back and forth in his sandals, arms folded across his chest, and grinned. "This is certainly the most unusual reception we have received in all Canaan. Eskie, whose idea was this?"

"Sir?"

"I understand about the show of force and the demonstration of marksmanship with that longbow. Very impressive. Even the food—with the 'quickest way to a man's heart' and all that. But who thought of gifts for the men's families?"

Eskie gulped. "Well, sir, the idea came from a lady friend of mine, a most unusual woman." He felt himself blush. *Maybe Joshua will not notice.*

Joshua turned, and his eyebrows went up. His grin broadened. "Her name is?"

Eskie wanted to sink into the ground. " 'Zalef. She made the pickled duck's eggs." *Aw, why did I say that? Eskie, shut up.*

"I see." Joshua turned back and continued to rock heel to toe, arms folded, grinning.

What did he see, but a young fool beside him?

"Seriously, though, where did you get your information about our father, Abraham?"

"That was from … my father, the potter of Gibeon. He spent a Sabbath recently with your high priest's son, learning from him."

"A most impressive man. How is your father?"

"Sir … we buried him four days ago. He was murdered."

Joshua's jaw dropped. "And Keshub does not know."

Eskie pressed his lips between his teeth and nodded. "I am hoping to see him go by today. I need to tell him."

"He is with Phinehas and the lead wagon. It will not be long before they arrive. I am sorry to hear of your father's death. I know Keshub will be devastated. I will release him for a fortnight to spend time at home."

"Thank you, sir, that is very kind of you."

* * *

The food and gifts carts already gone, Eskie stepped off the two-track gravel road as the first wagon came into view.

Joshua hailed Mr. Phinehas and spoke briefly to him, before Keshub stepped away and came to join Eskie. "Eskie! Joshua says I can spend a fortnight with family. It is good to see you."

Eskie tried to speak, but his voice would not come out.

"Eskie, is something wrong?"

Eskie got out, "Come." He put his arm over his little brother's shoulder and guided him to Naqib's shortcut to the top of Mount Moriah—eyes streaming. At the top of the climb, Eskie turned toward the wind coming in from the Negev. He combed back his hair with his fingers and again placed his arm across Keshub's shoulder—almost at the same level as his own.

Keshub, too, faced the hot desert wind and glanced Eskie's way. "Eskie, whatever it is I know, it must be bad, if you cannot talk. Is it Mamaa?"

Eskie shook his head side to side and cleared his throat. "Baba."

Keshub gasped. "What?"

"He is gone. … Ragar escaped the wood camp. … He came to our spring … and lay in wait for whoever came to the spring first that morning."

"Baba hardly ever goes to the spring early in the morning."

"He did three days ago."

Keshub struggled to speak. "Where is Ragar?"

"Dead. Samir and I followed him to the livery stable here. We got him. I will tell you about it later." Eskie embraced his brother. They wept together.

* * *

Eskie pointed to the wall, still manned by archers all around, until the last Hebrew passed through the Kidron Valley below. "Let's go into Jerusalem the back way from here. Maybe we will see Jebus or Jozman, the leader of the Jebusites. I need to let them know I will be going back to Gibeon for a few days."

"Certainly."

"Eskie!" A female voice.

He turned. 'Zalef stood on the height of the bald, limestone threshing floor, inactive today. He saw 'Raunah among the old men in the serving line. "Keshub, I have someone I would like you to meet." He rubbed his face with the tail of his girdle and combed his hair with his hands.

" 'Zalef, this is my brother Keshub. He is Joshua's servant. He travels with Joshua and his army."

'Zalef dipped her chin. "I am very glad to meet you, Keshub. You have a very brave brother." She glanced at Eskie and went on, "I am sure he has told you about your father by now. My deepest regrets for you and your loss. I wish I could have met him—such a great man by all reports of those who have met him."

"Thank you." Keshub acknowledged her words and turned to Eskie. "I will wait over there by the back gate."

"Thanks, brother." Eskie turned back to 'Zalef. "So Jebus has told you all that has been happening?"

"Yes." Her dark eyes traced his face. Her lashes swept her cheeks.

Eskie cleared his throat. "I am glad to see you before I leave."

"How long will you be gone?"

"Not long. A few days. Joshua knew our father. He granted Keshub a fortnight of leave. He was most kind."

"May I go too?" Her eyes still down, eyelashes flicking nervously.

Eskie's head snapped back. "You want to go to Gibeon?"

"Yes, my baba is busy here in Jerusalem. We have a house here now. And now that the siege is over, I am sure my cousin, Jalil, can go with us. ..." She raised her eyes to his. "It has been a very long while since I had a mother. I would like to get to know yours."

Shocked, Eskie could think of nothing to say, but blurted. "What about your ducks? And ... and ..."

She chuckled and took his elbow. "Perhaps you will take me to visit them one day, too."

"Judah
could not dislodge the
Jebusites …
In Jerusalem …"
JOSHUA 15:63

"The Benjamites …
Failed to dislodge the
Jebusites,
Who were living in
Jerusalem."
JUDGES 1:21

DISCUSSION QUESTIONS

1. Have you ever helped a friend who was injured? What were you able to do?

2. Eskie had a talent for hunting and helped his family by going hunting when there was a need. How have you helped your family accomplish a family goal? Or how do you contribute to the success of your family?

3. Have you experienced a death in your family? If you were close to the person who died, what is your best memory of that person?

4. How important would you say being "on time" is to you? What would you say are the benefits of being on time?

5. When have you experienced peer pressure? When have you said no to or avoided confrontation about doing something you consider wrong?

6. Have you ever been lost? How did you feel? How did you find your way?

7. Have you ever made a friend of a person so shy they would never have made the first attempt to get acquainted? How did that work out? What did you learn from that person?

8. Have your words ever gotten you in trouble? What did you learn from the problem your words caused?

9. If you have sibling(s), how well do you get along with your sibling(s)? How much time do you spend with your sibling(s)? What do you generally do together?

10. How have you changed or grown in the last year? Where do you see yourself being in five years?

BIBLIOGRAPHY

Some of the Internet Research Links Used

7/28/18 SMALL TREES/PROFUSE BLOOMS IN JULY/
JERUSALEM
https://www.dailynews.com/2014/07/10/the-flowers-of-july-
from-the-gold-medallion-tree-to-angel-trumpets/ From *Los
Angeles Daily News* Home/Garden page. JOSHUA SISKIN,
AUTHOR Joshua Siskin's website at www.thesmartergardener.
com.

6/16/18 PEPPERMINT TEA FOR INFLAMMATION: https://
eunatural.com/8-herbal-teas-to-help-beat-inflammation/

6/12/18 SPIDER WEB AS TINDER https://www.youtube.com/
watch?v=_eJ59iGqPNU

2/17/18 WHAT DOES AN EAGLE'S SCREAM SOUND LIKE?
https://www.youtube.com/watch?v=IdFxnbZtu1I

2/16/18 IBEX HABITS Female Ibex is nanny. Male is billy.
Females and males are in separate herds that come together only
to mate. Both have horns.
https://www.livescience.com/28102-ibex.html

1/12/18 WHERE IS A DUCK'S VOICE BOX? Answer: a male
duck does not have a voice box; thus he makes a wheezing sound,
not a quack.
https://books.google.com/books?id=DBw__rjJe4IC&p-
g=PA257&lpg=PA257&dq=Where+in+a+duck%27s+neck+

is+his+voice+box?&source=bl&ots=zwMxuSSU9q&sig=dS-8FouTSP9pxB4o8CdPwdCf_1rs&hl=en&sa=X&ved=0ahUKEw-jkkJ7K-L7WAhXny1QKHfagAoEQ6AEIPDAH#v=onep-age&q=Where%20in%20a%20duck's%20neck%20is%20his%20voice%20box%3F&f=false

12/28/17 CANAANITE (JEBUSITE) WALL AND TOWER.
Protects Gihon Spring from attack on city in Late Bronze Age.
Cave close by. www.biblewalks.com/Sites/Gihon.html

Other Resources:

Bernstein, Burton. *Sinai: The Great and Terrible Wilderness.* New York: Viking Press, 1979.

Bullinger, E. W. *The Witness of the Stars.* Grand Rapids, MI: Kregel Publications, 1967; Reprint of 1893 edition.

Gascoigne, Bamber. "History of Counting Systems and Numerals." *HistoryWorld.* www.historyworld.net/wrldhis/PlainTextHistories.asp?historyid=ab34

Gower, Ralph. *The New Manners and Customs of Bible Times.* Chicago: Moody Press, 1987.

Grimshaw, PhD, John *The Gardener's Atlas: The Origins, Discovery, and Cultivation of the World's Most Popular Garden Plants.* Willowdale, Ontario: Firefly Books, Ltd., 2002.

Magic and Medicine of Plants. Pleasantville, New York: The Reader's Digest Association, Inc.: 1986.

Marcy, Randolph B., Captain (U. S. Army). *The Prairie Traveler: A Handbook for Overland Expeditions.* Bedford, Massachusetts: Applewood Books, 1993. (Originally published 1859.)

Merrill, C., J. I. Packer, and William White Jr. The Bible Almanac: *A Comprehensive Handbook of the People of the Bible and How They Lived.* Nashville: Thomas Nelson Publishers, 1980.

Palestine: Country Report to the FAO International Technical Conference on Plant Genetic Resources. Leipzig, 1996.

Pritchard, James B. *Gibeon: Where the Sun Stood Still.* Princeton: Princeton University Press, 1962.

Pritchard, James B. *The Harper Atlas of the Bible.* New York: Harper & Row, 1987.

Rockefeller Museum, Jerusalem. Middle to Late Bronze Age, Exhibit #976. Flint Sickle from Tell el-Ajjul, May 2010.

St. John, Robert. *Roll, Jordan Roll: The Life Story of a River and Its People.* Garden City, NY: Doubleday, 1965.

The Odyssey of Homer. S. H. Butcher and A. Lang, trans. The Harvard Classics. Eliot, Charles W., LL.D.

Tubb, Jonathan N. *Canaanites: Peoples of the Past.* London: The British Museum Press, British Museum Company Ltd., 2006.

Wood, Bryant. "The Walls of Jericho. Archeology Confirms: They Really Did Come A-tumbling Down." www.answersingenesis.org/articles/cm/v21/n2/the-walls-of-jericho

ABOUT THE AUTHOR

Peggy Miracle Consolver's stories emerge from her multiple years of reading through the Bible chronologically. Her fiction books speak to the reader from a deep point of view from the main characters' experiences. From amazing stories of the Bible, she fills in the gaps, where God is silent—and gives an eyewitness account. Her principal characters live the historical events in real time in the Late Bronze Age.

Many of her insights come from having grown up on a farm in a large family and from her knowledge of agriculture and horticulture.

Consolver began to write after a brush with breast cancer. Her granddaughter, at seven years old, told her, "Grammy, I want to write books when I grow up!" The author said to herself, "I thought the same thing when I was her age, but if I'm going to do that, I'd better get started!"

In 2010, the author joined an archaeological dig at Khirbet el Maqatir, just five miles from El Jib, the confirmed present-day site of ancient Gibeon. On a side trip with a Palestinian tour guide, the author visited Gibeon and stood on the summit, where her characters stood—and saw the outskirts of modern Jerusalem on the horizon.

On another trip to Israel in 2017, Consolver explored the environs of ancient Jerusalem, including the Waters of Nephtoah and the Hill of Evil Counsel. Somehow, indeed providentially from her point of view, these sites were preserved from the modern urban encroachment all around them. Ancient history that had taken place there leapt onto the written page.

Consolver's other interests are her grandchildren and gardening. She has hosted annual summertime cousins' camps for the past sixteen years. Some of the "camp" activities have been hiking, fishing, swimming, golfing, archery, visiting museums, volunteering at a ministry that provides shoes for orphans, and visiting a college campus.

Having taught Sunday School for thirty-seven years, Consolver is a women's Bible study leader in her church. She lives in Plano, Texas, with her husband, and with her children and grandchildren nearby.